THE
EINSTAAT
BRIEF

ISBN-13: 9781636960401
ISBN-10: 1636960405

Cover design by: Damonza.com
Printed in the United States of America

BLAKE BANNER

A HARRY BAUER THRILLER

THE
EINSTAAT
BRIEF

R

RIGHT HOUSE

ALSO BY BLAKE BANNER

I have a huge catalog of eBooks online, but am slowly turning them all into paperbacks. If you'd like to see what I have in paperback at this very moment, then please visit the following site.

www.blakerbanner.com/books

Thank you once again for reading my work!

———————

ONE

They came from all over Europe, and from North America. They called themselves the Einstaat Group, because the small village of Einstaat, on the border of Germany and Luxembourg, was where they had their first meeting, way back in 1950, in the wake of the Second World War, ostensibly for the purpose of cementing Anglo-American relations. Since then their purpose had evolved; into what, nobody but them knew.

The name was not official, because the Einstaat Group was not any kind of official body. It was just an informal name—a useful handle—that had stuck. They had a steering committee who arranged the annual Einstaat Meetings, and that was co-chaired by the eminent Belgian economist Marcus Hoffmeister, and billionaire entrepreneur Anne-Marie Karrión. Who the members of the steering committee were, aside from the chairman and chairwoman, was a better-kept secret than what the Freemasons did with their balloons and aprons. What happened to anyone who spilled the beans was an equally well-kept secret.

Another, even better-kept secret was what they talked about at those meetings. The theory was that they talked about how to maintain world peace, freedom and democracy—those cornerstones of Anglo-American society. Back in 1950 everybody was worried that the United States and Russia would slide helplessly into a third world war, and the Europeans were especially worried that they would provide the battleground. So a small group of what was left of Continental Europe's aristocracy got together and had a quiet chat with General Walter B. Smith, the director of the CIA, who in turn had a quiet chat with General Marshal and advised him to advise Truman to hold private talks with Peter Zeeland, an exiled Polish politician, and Prince Joseph Alexander of Belgium. Some said that Prince Philip of the United Kingdom was also there. Others said he came in later. But the gist of that very private conversation was that it would be helpful to create a British-American axis of power to protect Western interests in the world, and to that end it would be a good idea to hold a weeklong, informal meeting once a year, at a different, undisclosed venue on each occasion, and invite the most eminent and influential heads of state, politicians, business leaders, academics and scientists of the day to attend. The meetings themselves would not be secret, but whatever went on at them, and whatever was discussed, would be. That way the attendees could enjoy total freedom of expression, and have fully frank and open discussions.

And so it happened that the Einstaat Group was born, and with it the conspiracy theory that this small, elite gang used it as a kind of AGM to run the world. According to that theory, they got together and planned wars, economic recessions, the price of oil, pandemics —you name it, they conspired to make it happen, and all for the benefit of that small elite. Naturally it was a crazy idea. Who the hell would believe that if you got the

Western world's richest, most powerful men and women together in a luxury hotel for a week, with no reporters and a no-holds-barred policy, that they would plot and conspire to exploit world events in their own interest?

Naturally, since the '90s, guests invited to attend had increasingly included dot-com billionaires and, above all, software developers. And since the new millennium, those software developers had increasingly included experts in the fields of social media and what had come to be known as "Strong AI": that branch of artificial intelligence that holds that consciousness is nothing but a set of really complicated algorithms, and all we need in order for computers and robots to develop sentience is a software that is complex and sophisticated enough to contain such algorithms.

So they came, one hundred and thirty guests from twenty-three countries: heads of state, captains of industry, economists and financiers, academics and scientists, from all over Europe and North America, to the tiny Principality of Andorra in the Pyrenees, nestled between Spain to the south and France to the north. Among the subjects for discussion that year, at the sixty-eighth meeting, were: a Stable Strategic Order, the Future of Europe, Brexit and Morality and Artificial Intelligence,

Given the topics for discussion it was no surprise that William Hughes, the software giant, was on the guest list, along with Andrew Ashkenazi, the social media mogul, rated by *Forbes* at the age of thirty-two as one of the ten most powerful men in the world, and Steve Plant, creator of the SearchEngine, a veritable software empire that had effectively shaped the late twentieth and early twenty-first centuries.

They had taken over the Grand Continental, a

super-luxury five-star hotel, for the week. It was situated on the edge of the Grandvalira Golf Course, near the tiny ski town of Soldeu. The hotel was closed to the public and the press, and a cordon of local cops, Europol, CIA and French and Spanish secret service had put the place on total lockdown three days before the guests had started to arrive

Andrew Ashkenazi, the creator of MyPal, was among the first to arrive, driving himself in a bright red, customized Aston Martin DBS Superleggera. He pulled up on the gravel drive outside the hotel lobby: a vast, sweeping gable in dark wood, faced with enormous sheets of bronzed plate-glass that reflected the green, snow-tipped peaks as though they were a dimly seen parallel universe.

He threw his keys to the waiting valet and strode toward the doors, creating a small, oddly menacing black silhouette against the vastness of the reflected mountains. He moved like a man who owned the world. He almost did.

A small group of hotel staff were waiting to greet him: Eugenio Costas, the hotel manager, and five pretty women in hotel uniforms. Men like Ashkenazi are not required to check in, show documentation or sign anything less momentous than a billion-dollar deal. They have people to do all that for them. All men like Ashkenazi have to do is demand. So Costas, a man with a shiny bald head and a blue blazer with brass buttons, bowed.

"Mr. Ashkenazi, may I say what an honor..."

Ashkenazi, a man in 501s and a Harvard sweatshirt, with nearly a hundred billion dollars in the bank, cut him short.

"Sure, it's nice to be here. Did my things arrive this morning?"

"They did, and your PA, Ms. Fenninger, has taken care of them. May we offer you…?"

"What about William Hughes? Has he arrived yet?"

"He is in the Emperor Suite, Mr. Ashkenazi. He has asked whether you would join him when you arrive, after you have rested…"

"Get me a Coke. You…" He pointed to one of the pretty girls in uniform. "Take me to his suite." She led the way across the marble floor toward an arch that gave onto a cobbled path, a wooden bridge and abundant, green gardens. She smiled at the thirty-two-year-old billionaire, while Costas issued orders for the urgent dispatch of a can of Coke to William Hughes's suite on the upper slope.

The girl and Ashkenazi followed a wending, cobbled path past weeping willows, over rustic bridges and among more gardens until they eventually came to the Emperor Suite. As she knocked and opened the door, Andrew Ashkenazi smiled at her.

"Make yourself available. What's your name? I'm going to ask for you personally if I need help with my bath, or pulling down the sheets."

The pretty girl giggled and said her name was Begonia and she would be happy to help with anything he needed. With which she left and closed the door behind her.

The Emperor Suite had a broad, galleried entrance occupied only by a sixteenth-century French credenza and a large mirror. Beyond the wooden balustrade, down three shallow steps, there opened out a spacious room with polished hardwood floors, minimalist white leather and suede armchairs and sofas and a square, copper fireplace that occupied the center of the floor. Randomly scattered bearskins littered the floor. The far wall, like the entrance to the building, was composed of vast sheets of plate-glass, and overlooked a deep, green valley, half-smothered in dense pine forests.

William Hughes had been sitting on one of those suede sofas, and now he stood and smiled in spite of himself. To him Ashkenazi looked like a child and privately, to him, his success seemed in some way obscene. But to Ashkenazi, Hughes looked old and tired. With his thin hair and liver spots on his temples and hands, to Andy Ashkenazi he was a relic and belonged in a museum, along with Windows 1.1 and Word Perfect. His smile looked weak. But he spread his arms, laughed and shook his head.

"What?" he said, "What is it with you? You own the One Ring of Power or something? You never grow any older?" Hughes laughed and Ashkenazi trotted down the steps. They embraced. "I used to read articles about you when I was fourteen. You look exactly the same now."

"Yeah?" Hughes laughed some more. "That's because you were fourteen last week." He pointed to a chair. "Sit down. Shall I tell you my secret? My secret is to eat less red meat, meditate regularly and only meet with very short-sighted people."

Ashkenazi didn't laugh. He smiled and grunted. "You had this place swept by your people?"

"And so have you. We can talk freely, Andrew."

There was a knock at the door and the pretty girl in uniform, named Begonia, entered with a silver tray, a glass of ice and lemon and a can of Coke. Both men watched her in silence as she opened the can, poured the drink and left. When she had gone, Ashkenazi said, "OK, tell me, no bullshit, no stories, no runarounds. When will it be ready?"

Hughes smiled. "It's ready now, but what we need is a system of delivery." He gestured at Ashkenazi with an open hand. "Have *you* got that? Last I heard you were ready to provide us with a delivery system."

"Delivery is not a problem..."

Hughes made a face like an indulgent parent and shook his head.

"No, see? This is why I find it so hard to trust you. You're a slippery snake, Andrew."

"Ha! Feel free to insult me! I'm just a jumped up little Jewish kid."

"I don't care if you're a Japanese geisha. You're a slippery bastard, Andrew. You know what 'Delivery is not a problem' tells me?"

"I know *you're* going to tell *me*."

"It tells me you have not arranged delivery of the product, and you are trying to manipulate the launch in a way that benefits you."

"Don't be so damned suspicious, Will!"

William Hughes grunted. "It seems to me you have a long track record of screwing over partners who should have been a little more suspicious of you. I'm not going to make a moral judgment, Andrew, but you should know that I am not about to make the same mistake as all those other people you screwed. You don't get sight, sound or smell of the product until I see that delivery is firmly in place."

Ashkenazi leaned forward and stared at William Hughes for a moment before reaching for his glass.

"Delivery is one hundred percent in place."

Hughes shook his head. "I don't want a fucking virus, Andrew."

"You're not going to get one. You're going to get what you asked for."

"It has to recycle itself…"

"It will do more than that, Will. It will integrate itself into the very fabric of the virtual world. It will become the DNA of the entire global network."

Hughes did not look satisfied. He gave a small sigh. "Delivery is everything, Andrew."

Andrew Ashkenazi shrugged and spread his hands. "What's wrong with you? What more do you want? What better than the world's largest social media platform? There is hardly a person, physical or fiscal, on the whole planet who isn't a member, and there sure as hell isn't a business. Not in the West. And you know as well as I do that we can creep in the back doors of the Eastern networks."

"That's theory, Andrew. Have you got an actual, operational delivery system?"

"Yes."

"Good." He didn't beam. His face just said he was satisfied. "Then we only have to fix a date. We can discuss it with our partners this evening. What was the other thing you wanted to discuss with me?"

Andrew Ashkenazi picked up his glass and drained half of it. He smacked his lips as he set it down and said, as though he was talking to the glass, "A few of our friends got killed."

Hughes didn't say anything. He just gave a small nod. Ashkenazi went on:

"Mary Jones…"

"That's it. Just Mary Jones."

Ashkenazi made a face like he was being patient. "OK," he said. "She's the only *real* friend…"

Hughes interrupted him again. "And she might well have been killed by the Chinese. She went bad."

"They say not."

"Of course they do. When have you ever known the Chinese to tell the truth? I don't like this paranoia, Andrew. It is not healthy. I'm getting reports that you are talking like this to other people."

"Yeah, Will, because something has to be done."

"Something, like what?"

"Like at the very least we need to look into it."

Will Hughes shrugged and spread his hands. "Look into what, for Pete's sake? Mary was playing a very dangerous game, double-crossing everybody. She was going to get killed sooner or later. And besides, it played out for us in the end. We got the vaccine."

"Forgive me for being blunt, Will, but you're being really shortsighted. It's not just her death. It's the very fact that we *did* get the vaccine. How the hell did the Navy know the vaccine was on the *Chénxīng*? How did they know it was on that *particular* ship? Where did they get that information from, Will?"

"I don't know."

Ashkenazi stood and walked to the vast glass wall overlooking the deep green valley. "There is something else," he said, without looking back. "I have sources that say her operation in Morocco was destroyed."

"Yeah, by the Moroccan government."

Now he turned to face Hughes. "Why would they do that? They stood to make a killing if they backed her. I'm telling you, Will, somebody is interfering. I want to know who, and why."

Hughes was quiet for a long while, then he pulled a cell phone from his jacket pocket and dialed a number. It rang a couple of times before he smiled and spoke.

"Gina, how are you, sweetheart...? Sure, sure... Well, you know, I'm trying to look after myself, less red meat, cutting down on the alcohol, trying to enjoy life more, the small, good things, you know what I'm talking about..."

He waited a moment, listening, nodding, smiling.

"Well, that's right, Gina. That exactly it. There's gotta be more than work, right? Listen, I'm here at Soldeu..." He laughed. "Einstaat Week, that's right. Yeah, you'll get the report. And anyway, we were just talking about Mary Jones. You remember her? That's the one, black, beautiful, all the way up legs..." He laughed at something Gina said, then went on. "Thing is, Gina, I'm hearing that there are rumors..."

He went quiet again, listening. After a bit he glanced at Ashkenazi and said into the phone, "Their room at the Mandarin Oriental? Really? And, here's the sixty-million-dollar question: do you know how the Navy got to know it was the *Chénxīng* carrying the vaccine?"

He listened some more and started frowning.

"Mohamed Ben-Amini? But he was not a friend... Oh he was? You'd turned him? Shit... You got any ideas who it might be?"

He leaned back in the sofa, crossed one long leg over the other and listened for a good three or four minutes without speaking. Then he said, "OK, Gina, thanks. Listen, you should come over, spend the weekend. I'll call you when I get back. Yeah, you take care."

He hung up and Ashkenazi said, "So?"

"The Firm are aware that there may be somebody interfering."

"Who?"

"They don't know. They think it may be an internal agency. She thinks we could cooperate."

"Shit."

"Shit's right, and we have to make sure it doesn't hit the fan. They have an individual they are looking at. They have tabs on him and they're hoping he'll lead them to whoever he works for."

"Who?"

"A guy called Harry Bauer, ex British SAS. Resigned under peculiar circumstances. Returned to New York, has no obvious source of income but lives well. Travels abroad sometimes."

He pressed a buzzer on the table and after a moment a door opened in the far right wall. A man in black pants and a white jacket came in and bowed.

"Whiskey. Get a bottle of Black Label, ice..." He made an inquiring face at Ashkenazi and on receiving a nod said, "Two glasses."

When the flunky had gone Ashkenazi said, "We need to know who he is, or who they are. We need to know who the fuck is doing this and what they want. And why the fuck the Agency isn't protecting us!"

"Don't panic, Andrew. I'll put some people on it. We'll get to the bottom of this, and snuff it out."

Ashkenazi studied Hughes's face a while, then nodded.

"You'd better, old man. You'd better."

That was the way I heard it, much later.

TWO

She had red hair and freckles. Not many women can pull that off, but she could. She also had dark blue eyes that seemed to smile on their own. But when her mouth joined in, she had dimples too. Her name was Kate, and she was from Texas.

We were sitting on the warm, stone steps at the Central Park Reservoir. She was eating an ice-cream cone and kept glancing at me. The sun was bright among dappled shadows on her pale skin.

"How many dates is this now, Harry?"

"I don't know. I lost track. The last few all just kind of blended in to one because you refuse to go home."

She stopped eating and looked at me, her eyes flitting over my face to see if I was serious. I smiled to show I wasn't.

"You want me to go?"

I was kind of surprised to realize I didn't. "No," I said. "I've grown accustomed to your face."

"Is that supposed to be a compliment?"

"It's an easy face to get accustomed to, so I guess it is."

She went back to her ice cream.

"Don't get too accustomed. You don't want to take

me for granted. Texas farm girls don't take too kindly to that."

It was eleven in the morning and the crowds of visitors and tourists were growing thicker. A guy on a skateboard rattled past me, inches away, and I watched him jump on the rail and slide down. I said:

"You want to walk?"

"Sure." She stood and took my hand. "You're kind of tense. You OK?"

We started walking, flanking the reservoir, keeping the water on our left, moving north. After a moment I smiled at her again.

"I'm OK. I'm not tense. What's on your mind? Why'd you ask about how many dates?"

She didn't answer for a while. Instead she gazed out at the small glinting waves: a glare of light on one side, black on the other. She squeezed my hand and leaned gently against me as we walked. Eventually she said, without looking at me, "You know, I don't want to stereotype, but at heart I am just a plain, old-fashioned Texas country girl." She paused and looked up at me. Her eyes were uncertain, searching. "I've been in New York for two years, but I have not really become a New Yorker. Do you know what I mean, Harry?"

"I know what you mean. I don't know what you're driving at."

She screwed up her face and sighed, then looked away again at the water. After that it was at her feet as she walked.

"I guess, you guys..."

"Y'all?"

She laughed. "Yeah, y'all, are kind of free and easy, you hook up, hang out and move on. You go on a date, like each other and hit the sack. I'm not saying that's wrong..."

"You don't do that in Texas?"

"Don't tease me, Harry. Sure, in Dallas and Houston and Austin. In the cities I guess people are more liberal. Half of 'em ain't Texan anyhow. But mostly we have our feet pretty firmly on the ground."

I stopped walking and turned to face her under the shade of the trees. A couple of people jostled past and I moved her over to the rails overlooking the water.

"Are you asking me what my intentions are? Shouldn't your dad be asking me that, while he polishes his Colt revolvers?"

"Don't make it sound stupid, Harry."

"That's not my intention. I like that you're asking me."

"It's been a month now, since we started seeing each other, and half that time we've been pretty much living together. I guess we know each other pretty well by now."

I nodded. "We do, I guess."

"Am I scaring you? Have I screwed things up?"

"No. No, not at all."

"What is it, then?"

"It is very difficult for me to explain..."

"Is there another woman?"

I laughed. "No, no, there is no other woman. If only it were that simple."

Her forehead clenched like a fist. "Well, what is it then, Harry?"

I turned away, feeling suddenly ashamed and humiliated. How do you explain to a kind, humane woman that you kill people for a living? That that's the only thing you know how to do well? I leaned my elbows on the iron rail and looked down at the small, lapping waves, silver and black. She came up close beside me and put one hand on my arm.

"It's my work," I said, and heard how lame it sounded.

"Your *work*? Well, now, that sounds like a real poor excuse!"

"No." I shook my head. "It's not an excuse, Kate. I have to travel quite a bit, at short notice..."

"Well, shoot! I don't mind that." Her face lit up. "Especially if I can come along sometimes!"

The thought of it made me smile. "My work is quite dangerous, sometimes."

"Dangerous? How dangerous?"

I took a deep breath and held it for a moment. "It's very specialized..."

"Like working on an oil rig?"

"Something like that. Sometimes the locations can be...uncomfortable."

She was frowning hard now. "I don't know why you're being so cagey. Let me ask you something, Harry."

I looked at her and waited. She held my eye.

"What were you planning to do? What did you think was going to happen with us? You thought one day you'd go off to your work and when you got back you simply wouldn't call? And that would be the end of Kate?"

"No!" I shook my head with feeling. "No, not at all!"

"Well, what then?"

"I hadn't thought that far ahead. I had avoided thinking about it. Sometimes I just take things one day at a time..."

"Well, this girl ain't a one day at a time kind of girl."

"I know that."

"So...?"

I put my arm around her and started to walk again.

"I've been thinking for a while now that I should leave my job."

"*Leave* your *job?* You can do that? My word, Harry! I don't want you to leave your job on account of me! What would you live on?"

"I've been thinking about it for a while, Kate. Before we met."

"Don't you like your work? What would you do instead?"

"It's..." I smiled grimly at the leaves overhead, at the people passing by in their infinite variety. "Sometimes it is very satisfying. But it's draining too. I am very tired."

She pulled away slightly, still holding my arm, and frown-smiled at me.

"You are being *awful* mysterious! You don't work for the CIA, do you? Or the FBI, or the NSA?"

"No, Kate. I am not a spy and I am not a federal agent. It's nothing like that. I just have a dangerous job that keeps me away from home sometimes. But I'll tell you what I'm going to do."

I stopped and took a hold of her shoulders in my hands. She felt small and fragile, and I suddenly desired her intensely. Her face lit up as she looked up into mine, and her eyes were incredibly blue.

"What?" She gave a small, childlike laugh.

"I'm going to talk to my boss today. I'm going to give him notice. I'm going to quit my job."

She frowned, cocked her head on one side.

"Harry? Are you serious? You're going to quit your

job so we can be together? Isn't that a bit weird? I have to tell you, you got me a bit worried. I can't afford to keep us both..."

I laughed. "I know that. And it's not weird."

"What are we going to live on?"

"Oh," I shrugged and shook my head, "I'm OK financially. I guess I don't really need to work."

She was still frowning. "Seriously? You don't need to work?"

"Yeah, come on." I took her arm and we started walking again. But she was resistant and kept hanging back. I said, "I made a lot of money in my time. I can take early retirement."

She stopped and I stopped to turn to face her. I frowned.

"I thought you'd be pleased, Kate."

"I guess I might be if you weren't so mysterious. Harry, are you involved in some kind of crime? Are you a gangster or something?"

"No."

"Then why can't you tell me what you do?"

I sighed, looked out over the reservoir for a moment, sucking my teeth, then made up my mind.

"Kate, you know what a confidentiality agreement is, right?"

"Of course."

"Well, I work for a company that deals in huge sums of money, millions, tens of millions, and sometimes they need a tough guy like me to troubleshoot for them. Now, if you're troubleshooting a problem in LA, or Washington, it's no big deal. You just talk tough and look mean. But if you have a problem on a pipeline in Baghdad or Thailand, then it's not enough to talk tough. Things can get pretty dangerous. And believe me, these people take their confidentiality agreements very seriously. So I can't tell you the details."

She made a big round O with her mouth and nodded a few times. Then she took my arm and we started to walk again.

"So how come you're such a tough guy?"

"Well, I can tell you that. That's not a secret. I was in a special ops regiment in the UK."

"You were a soldier? Like the SEALs?"

"Yeah, for eight years. We were in Iraq and I did a lot of work in Afghanistan."

"So you've shot and killed people."

I didn't answer for a while. Eventually I said, "Yes, Kate. I have killed men. Is that a problem?"

She gave a nervous laugh and there were colored spots on her cheeks. "Hey! I'm from Texas, remember? I like my boys tough. And I guess that's why they paid you so well."

"There are perks to the job, yeah."

"I bet. You sure you're ready to give it up? A man can get addicted to that kind of life."

I looked into her big blue eyes for a long time before answering. I was remembering Iraq, the dismembered bodies in the dust by the roadside, the torture and murder in the jungles of Colombia and Mexico, the massacre at Al-Landy in Afghanistan. And above all, the rampage of murder I had embarked upon since I'd left the Regiment.

"I'm sure," I said. "It's time for a change." I smiled. "You want to buy a ranch in cowboy country? We could raise horses, cattle and kids."

She put her arms around me and held me real

tight. And I held her back. After a moment I held her face in my hands and tilted it up to mine.

"Listen, let's do something. Instead of lunch, let's buy some pizzas. We'll go to your place, collect your stuff and arrange a removal company to come and get the rest..."

Her cheeks flushed and she went on tiptoes.

"Really? Oh man! But my furniture. It won't all fit in your house..."

"We'll put it in storage till we find a bigger place."

"In New York?"

"You want to move? You want to go back to Texas? California? Wyoming?"

"Wyoming? Oh my god! I *love* Wyoming!"

"You want to look for a ranch in Wyoming?"

She leapt and hung on my neck and I laughed and held her while she squealed like a kid and kicked her feet.

We drove back to her place. She had a small, detached house on Hollywood Avenue, near Locust Point, which she'd rented from a friend of her parents while she got settled, teaching at the Villa Maria Academy. We spent the afternoon loading up my Jeep and ferrying over the stuff she wanted to take with her, while she telephoned removal companies and storage companies and got the bulkier furniture ready for collection the next day.

By eight PM we were pretty much done and Kate put a cold beer in my hand, dropped on the sofa and grinned at me.

"You mind if we stay the night here?"

"You don't like my house?"

"Your house is cute, but what can I tell you? I'm sentimental. I've been here a whole month and..." She shrugged. "I'd just like to say goodbye. We can cook something nice, get some wine..."

"All your pots and pans are at my place..."

"So we'll get takeout. Better still, it's a twenty-minute stroll to Paddy's, down on Pennyfield Avenue. They do draught beer and burgers. We'll chill there, then stroll back here for dessert."

She winked and I smiled. "What the hell are we waiting for?"

"I'm going to shower. And you..." She stood and gave me a lingering kiss. "...you have a think about packing in your job. I want you to be sure about what you're doing, mister. And, remember this: as long as I *know* what you're doing, you don't need to stop doing it if you don't want to. Stand by your man, and all that."

She kissed me again and went up to the shower.

We spent the evening relaxing by the river, drinking beer and eating burgers with hot chili sauce, and talking about possible things we could do with our future lives. It was an odd and novel feeling for me, but it was something I felt I could get used to pretty quickly.

By the time we left it was gone twelve and the streets were very quiet. It had been a short walk coming, but now it seemed like a long, dark walk back. The trees were abundant and obscured a lot of the houses on the left side of the road. The streetlamps, bolted to wooden poles, cast a dim, limpid yellow light, and the only sound aside from a desultory foghorn on the river was the crunch of our feet.

Behind us I heard the low hum of an engine. I turned and looked, vaguely aware that I hadn't heard the slam of a car door. Headlamps approached and I eased Kate onto the sidewalk. A dark Audi cruised past and was swallowed by the diminishing glow of its own lights.

I felt a tug on my arm and her hand on my chest.

"You *are* tense. You sure you're OK?"

"Sure. Old habits." I smiled.

We arrived at her place fifteen minutes later. The streets were still and quiet, and the sound of her key in the lock was surprisingly loud. While she opened the door into the dark house I scanned the street. The light was poor, all the drapes in all the windows were closed, and the yellow lamplight reflected dully on the black windshields of the Fords, Buicks and Hondas, and on one dark Audi. It was hard to tell, with the lamplight reflected bronze on the windshield, whether there was anybody in it or not.

A snap behind me told me Kate had put on the hall light. I turned and climbed the stairs, went inside and closed the door behind me. She smiled at me and placed both her palms on my chest.

"You go up and get ready for bed. I have a little surprise for you."

I raised an eyebrow. "I'm not used to pleasant surprises. What is it?"

"Just something I got while you were delivering my books and my bedding. Don't be so uptight. I'll be up in a second."

She disappeared toward the bathroom and I climbed the stairs to the bedroom. As I stripped for the shower I peered out of the window. The Audi was still there, and the copper reflection of the streetlamp still made it impossible to see inside. I figured maybe Kate was right and I was being paranoid, but like I'd told Kate, old habits die hard, and the careless die young.

I stood under the shower for five minutes. While I was toweling myself dry I heard the bedroom door open and close, a soft clunk as of something heavy being laid down. I pulled on my pants and opened the door.

She was sitting on the bed in a transparent negligee. On the bedside table there was an ice bucket and in it there was a bottle of Moet Chandon French champagne, and two champagne flutes chilling in the ice.

She smiled and her cheeks colored.

"You gonna make it pop, tough guy?"

That was when I heard the door open downstairs.

THREE

I pointed at Kate and mouthed, "Stay there." Then I killed the lights and closed the drapes.

One step took me to my bedside table. The drawer was polished and oiled and slid open noiselessly. I took out my Fairbairn & Sykes fighting knife, and my Sig Sauer P226. I knew it was loaded because I always keep it loaded. Just like I keep all the hinges in my house oiled, except the front and back doors. I want to hear anybody coming in. I don't want them to hear me coming down to get them.

I cocked the Sig and knelt beside the door, trained the weapon at where the intruder's belly would be if he had climbed the stairs, and eased it open. I knew, because I had run the simulation a dozen times in my mind over the last month, that there would be enough filtered light from the bathroom window, and from the living room window downstairs, for me to see a body on the stairs or on the landing. But the bedroom would be nothing but a black hole.

There was nothing to see. But there was a soft creak from the third stair from the bottom. I stood and took one long, silent step to the banisters and looked over. There was one guy in black with a balaclava over his head.

He had a semiautomatic in his hand and he was standing immobile, waiting, listening. I waited and listened with him. I was aware of just one guy, but that didn't mean there weren't more down there.

He glanced back over his shoulder, made a gesture with his left hand and took another step. I smiled. There was at least one more, but I doubted there were more than three.

I vaulted the banister, twisting my body so I was facing down the stairs, and landed slamming my heels into the top of balaclava's head. I felt the crunch of his skull cracking under my bare feet, and the snap of his neck. His body yielded and toppled under my weight and I fell, crouching, toward the bottom of the stairs.

As I fell and rolled I caught a glimpse of a silhouette against the streetlight coming in through the living-room window. I saw the unmistakable flash of fire, then heard the spit and *phut!* of a suppressed weapon as two slugs thudded home into the wall behind me. That was followed by a muffled curse.

The thought flashed through my mind of returning fire, but the last thing I needed, if I could avoid it, was my neighbors calling the cops. So I grunted and stifled a cry, like I'd been hit, as I put the Sig in my waistband and slipped the hard, steel blade from my boot. Then I crouched and stormed across the dark room at the blackness where the shots had come from. Again two more flashes of hot light. Again the double, lethal spit of flame and the hot pop of air by my ear as the slugs flashed past.

Then there was the heavy, intimate contact of a large, hard body as we collided. I grabbed for his right wrist, intensely aware of the semiautomatic he was holding, expecting at every fraction of a second the fierce explosion and the scorch of the bullet. I felt the hot barrel in my hand and levered down savagely. And then a ton of bricks smashed into my face.

The pain was excruciating and for a moment a wave of nausea swept over me as my legs went to jelly. But I felt the pistol come away in my hand and whipped it hard across his face. He cursed. I stumbled forward another step and backhanded him with the butt of the semi-automatic. He roared in the darkness and I knew what was coming. So I ducked and stepped in close and to the side, willing my legs to respond, as two massive hooks tore the air above my head. Then he lashed out blindly with his right foot and his boot scraped my thigh. But it didn't hurt. The blood was pounding around my body again and I was ready to move in for the kill.

The great thing about the Fairbairn & Sykes fighting knife is not the razor-sharp double-edged, carbon steel blade, or the rutted, steel grip of the handle. It's the needle-sharp, tapered point. You don't need to exert any pressure, you don't need to stab. You just need to get up close and let him come at you.

And that was exactly what he did.

I whispered, "I'm here, asshole," and he came at me; and walked right onto the needle-sharp blade. It slid in effortlessly and for a moment he didn't even know he'd been stabbed, until I wrapped my left arm around his neck and levered the blade up, cutting through his liver and into his diaphragm. Then I eased him down to the floor.

I should have cut his thigh instead, or his underarm. I should have kept him alive and made him talk, made him tell me who the hell he was and who he worked for; why he had come to kill me. But in the dark, with

Kate's life at risk, I could not afford that luxury.

I left the lights off and checked the ground floor quickly. I peered out though the window. Everything was still and quiet. The Audi was still there, dark and motionless. I went to the kitchen and peered out into the backyard. There was nothing, nobody. So I sprinted up the stairs to the bedroom.

At the door I paused.

"Kate, it's me. It's all clear. I'm coming in. You OK?"

She didn't answer. I moved into the room. She wasn't in the bed. I froze, listening. I could just make out the stifled breath in the darker shadows beyond the bed.

"Kate, it's me, Harry. Everything's OK. I'm going to put on the light so you can see me."

I had the Sig in my hand, trained on the darkness where I could hear the stifled, shaky breath. I snapped on the light.

She was sitting on the floor, pressed into the corner clutching her knees. Her eyes were squeezed tight and her teeth were clamped onto her lower lip. I stepped over to the window, flattened myself against the wall and moved the drape an inch. There was still no movement in the street. The Audi was still there, with the amber light reflected on its windshield. Nothing had changed. Everything was still and quiet.

I turned back to Kate. She had opened her eyes and was staring at me, at my body, trembling. I went and hunkered down in front of her.

"It was a break-in. It's over. There is nothing for you to worry about. There is no danger. OK?"

She gave a small, terrified nod. I gave her my hand and pulled her gently to her feet, then sat her on the bed.

"I'm going to make a call. Are you OK?"

"Police?"

I hesitated for a fraction of a second. "Yeah, the police."

I went out on the landing and called Cobra. It rang once and a woman's voice said, "Please identify yourself."

"It's Dirty Harry. I need the cleaning service."

I knew I was being fed through voice recognition. There was a pause. Then, "Where was the spillage?"

I gave her the address and added, "I have two suits that have been stained with tomato ketchup. The carpet's been ruined."

"Has anybody else been notified?"

"No."

"Are you alone?"

"I'm with my girlfriend."

There was a sigh. "I'll have to notify Buddy."

"Yeah, I know."

I hung up and turned toward the bedroom again. She was standing in the doorway with her hands clenched in front of her belly. She was still trembling and her face was confused and scared.

"Harry, what's going on?"

"Nothing. You should stay in the bedroom until..."

"Who were you talking to? The police will want a statement from me."

I didn't answer. I couldn't answer.

"Why did you call yourself Dirty Harry? What is a cleaning service? Who are you, Harry?"

"I told you."

"No, you lied."

"I didn't..." I had to stop. The lie stuck in my throat. "I can't tell you. Don't ask me, Kate. I told you I was going to resign."

She looked past me at the stairwell.

"What did you do?"

"I did what I had to do to protect you."

"You killed them."

"What should I have done? Should I have let them kill me? Should I have let them climb the stairs and rape and kill you?"

She stared at me for a long moment. Her eyes were wide, uncomprehending. "I don't know who you are," she said.

I gripped her shoulders, feeling a hot pellet of anger and frustration burning in my belly. I snarled, "I am exactly who you thought I was this morning, goddammit!"

"You're scaring me."

I closed my eyes, took a deep breath.

"You don't need to be scared of me, Kate. I just put my life on the line to protect you."

She backed away a step. "If they had been burglars, if it had been a home invasion…"

"Maybe that's what it was…"

"But the phone call, who did you call, Harry? You said, 'I have two suits that have been stained with tomato ketchup. The carpet's been ruined.' What the hell, Harry…?"

I spoke savagely, my fingers biting into her shoulders:

"You can't know any of this! You can't be a part of this!"

"*But I am a part of it!*" Her eyes welled with tears and she bit her lip hard. "What you just did made me a part of it…"

I shook my head. "No, you have to go. Take the car.

Go to..."

"Harry, stop it! Just tell me what the *hell* is going on and who the *hell* you are!"

I closed my eyes and pulled her to me, holding her tight. "No, no, you mustn't know. It's over. I am ending it tonight. Just forget this...."

"*Forget it?*" she shouted and pushed away from me, staring into my eyes like I was crazy. "*Forget it? How the hell am I supposed to forget it?*"

Outside I heard the hum of a car turning into the street. It stopped and after a moment the door slammed.

"Stay here. Don't leave this room. Try and sleep."

I closed the door and went down the stairs to open the door. Captain Russ White was there in a Fedora hat and a trench coat. A cigarette poking out of his mouth said he still didn't care too much for what was socially acceptable in the twenty-first century. With him were two guys with dark eyes and olive skin, dressed in blue overalls and baseball caps. I said:

"Hello, Russ," and stood back to let them in.

He stepped over the threshold and stood in the gloom of the living room looking around, then turned to the boys standing in the doorway.

"It's a three," he said, and the boys turned and went back to the car. Russ went to the stairs and stared at the crumpled, broken body there.

"It's true what they say about you. You did this in the dark?"

"There was some light from the window."

He jerked his chin at the semi-disemboweled body on the floor, then pointed at my belly as he spoke.

"But you made an unholy mess with this guy."

"I couldn't see him. I had to take the breaks as they

came."

"You said there's a girl?"

"Upstairs."

"She seen the state you're in?" I didn't answer, re-membering her terrified eyes as she stared at me. "Is the NGO compromised?"

I scowled. "NGO?"

He arched an eyebrow. "Non-Governmental Organ-ization, Harry. Cobra. Are we compromised? Did you tell your friend upstairs anything?"

"No, of course not."

I heard a trunk slam outside and turned to watch the two boys struggling down the path with two cases of equipment. Russ watched me watching them and as they humped the stuff through the door he said:

"You know we don't hurt innocent people, Harry. But if she knows something—anything—we need to man-age it and limit the damage."

"She knows nothing. She knows I have skills and she knows I was in the British Army. That's it."

He moved across the room and into the open-plan kitchen as the guys dumped their equipment and went to work on the gutted body with a plastic sheet.

"Let's get ourselves out of the way and let them work. You have any whisky in this place? I seem to re-member you kept a fine Macallan..."

"Yeah." I reached in the kitchen cabinet and pulled out a bottle of Johnny Walker. "This isn't my house."

I paused and we stared at each other a moment. Then I took two glasses and spilled some whisky into each. He said:

"So this isn't your house. She knows you were in the SAS and you have the skills that go with that. That's it, but..."

He took a sip and smacked his lips.

"But what? But nothing."

"But there is something else. I have a sixth sense about this. I read people, Harry. That's my superpower. There is something else. What is it?"

I sipped my whisky, and as I rolled it around my mouth I stared into the glass and tipped it this way and that. It was as good as telling him he was right. I asked:

"You talk to the brigadier?"

"I live in his pocket. I take care of business, Harry. We talk every day. He doesn't sneeze without running it by me first. What's on your mind?"

"I'm going to quit, Russ. I want to get married, settle down, have a normal life."

He snorted. "A normal life? I hear people talk about that sometimes. I think I saw it in a movie once too. Something out of Hollywood."

"I didn't say a perfect life, Russ. Just a normal one, where I don't have to kill people for a living. Where I don't wind up at two in the morning drinking whisky in the kitchen, while two guys I never met remove dead bodies from my living room, and my girlfriend trembles in terror upstairs."

He set down his glass and reached in his breast pocket. "She's probably in shock. Give her one of these."

He handed me a small sheet with six tablets in it. I took it. "Thanks." Then I looked at him. "You think this is normal?"

He shrugged. "They told me there was a girl here. It'll help her get over the shock."

I took a glass and filled it with water. He watched me and added: "If you give it to her with a glass of whisky it will work faster. But make sure you cover her well. And wipe all that damned blood off of you before you go and see her again."

He grabbed a kitchen towel, screwed it up and threw it at me. I soaked it in water and poured washing-up liquid over it, then washed myself clean. When I was done he held out his hand for the towel. I gave it to him and climbed the stairs with the water and the tranquilizer.

FOUR

S he had taken the tablet gratefully and I had sat with her while she fell asleep. Then, after the guys had driven away with the bodies, presumably to dispose of them in the East River (I was not allowed to know), Russ had helped me to carry Kate down to my Jeep, and we had driven her home to my house. Now, as she slept in my bed, Russ and I sat, with the French doors open onto the backyard, each with a glass of the Macallan, talking in quiet voices. Russ, after a silence, had said to me:

"He won't be happy."

"I'm not doing it to make Brigadier Buddy Bird happy, Russ. I'm doing it to make me and Kate happy. He's had a couple of good hits out of me."

"Nobody's disputing that, Harry. On the contrary. That's exactly why he won't be happy. The job in Thailand was superb. Not many operatives could have pulled that off."

I smiled with more than a hint of irony. "You trying to flatter me?"

"Flattery is not something US Air Force captains are known for. But it is what it is. You pulled off a couple of damned good jobs. He's not going to like your resigning."

"Well, there's not a hell of a lot he can do about it except send me a wedding gift."

I saw his eyebrows climb his forehead.

"Really? It's that serious?"

"Yeah, it's that serious. I'm not comfortable talking about feelings. You know that. But she's special. She makes me feel human. I've saved some money. You know we get spoils?"

He nodded. "I've been there, Harry. I did the job for a couple of years."

"So you know. If there are spoils to be had, we get them. I've been lucky. Now I want to make a home..."

"White picket fence?" He smiled to show it wasn't sarcasm.

I shook my head. "A ranch, get married, have kids. Normal, Russ. Normal and healthy."

"He's going to want to talk to you. You know that."

"Yeah. I want to talk to him, too."

He sat staring at me for a long moment, holding my eye.

"He's going to want to know who those two guys were."

"That's what I want to know."

"It's a shame you didn't ask them. If you'd asked politely they might have told you."

"Like I said, it was dark, it was a surprise attack and my main concern was to neutralize the threat and protect Kate."

He nodded a few times, gazing out into the darkness of the backyard.

"It was a surprise attack," he said. "It was that, all right." He took a swig and swirled it around his mouth for a while, like he was tasting his own thoughts instead of the whisky. "He has a job for you," he said at last. "He's going to want you to do it."

I shook my head. "No. I want out. I promised Kate."

"It's a big job. It's an important job. He needs you to do it."

"You can tell him, I'm not going to do it."

He smiled at me. "I'm not going to tell him that. You can tell him that if you want to, but I'm not going to."

I sighed. "When?"

"Tomorrow." He saw my eyes glance toward the stairs. "We'll look after her. She'll be safe. But you know as well as I do they weren't after her. They were after you."

"I know that." I sighed again, more heavily. "Where? Do I have to go to the Manor?"

The Manor was what we had started calling Cobra HQ. It was an old manor house in Westchester, just outside Pleasantville.

"No," he said. "I don't think he'll want you to go there. He's going to view you as compromised right now."

"What the hell!" I felt a hot pellet of anger smolder in my belly. "I'm not compromised!"

He shrugged and made a "tell it to somebody else" face.

"You have divided loyalties right now. And you want to leave the group. That could make you a liability. I'd say you were compromised."

"Screw you!"

He drained his glass, put it on the table and made to stand. "I just got you out of a whole lot of trouble, pal. I wouldn't let that mouth of yours run away with you. Seems to me you need friends right now. The brigadier will be in touch in the next few hours. My advice? Meet him, talk with him, reach some kind of arrangement. If you opt out of the job, you're going to need some goodwill and some long-term protection, wherever you go to set up your normal family ranch." He raised the empty glass. "Thanks for the whisky."

He stood, picked up his hat and made his way to the door. As he reached for the handle I said, "I'm not compromised, Russ. Tell him. You know damn well I'm not."

He nodded in a way that was noncommittal and stepped out into the small hours of the morning. I heard his leather soles crunch on the sidewalk, and the rumble of his car as he fired up and drove away. Then there was silence, and after that the horizon started to turn a pale blue-gray, and the dawn chorus of the birds announced the new day.

At seven I went up to look at Kate. She was sleeping peacefully and looked like World War Three wouldn't wake her. So I went back down and made a pot of strong, black coffee, laced it with the Macallan—which I knew was a hanging offence in Scotland, but I didn't care right then—and toasted some rye bread.

At exactly eight o'clock my cell rang. I knew who it was.

"Yeah."

"Good morning, Harry, this is Buddy."

"I know."

"I've just been having breakfast with Captain Russ White. He told me he had been to see you to help with some housework."

"Are you born like that?"

"I beg your pardon?"

"The Brits, are you born like that, calling disposing of a disemboweled body 'housework'?"

"Can we try to stay on task, Harry?

"Whose task, Brigadier, yours or mine?"

"Either will do to start with, Harry. But I don't think it profits either of us if you sulk."

"Agreed."

"Also, I don't think this is a conversation I want to have on the telephone."

"But you don't want me at HQ, either."

"Not especially, no. And I have to say that is rather inconvenient."

"I am *not* compromised, sir!"

"That may well be what you believe, Harry. And I don't doubt your integrity. But we have no idea who this woman is, and furthermore, your loyalty is now divided. We'll meet at the Hyatt Place, in Flushing, on 39th Avenue. I'll see you in the bar at noon. Try and get some sleep before then."

"Yes, Mom." I hesitated a moment. "What about Kate? I can't leave her here alone."

"That rather illustrates my point, Harry, doesn't it? Like it or not, you have acquired a very vulnerable Achilles' heel." He gave that a second to sink in, then went on. "Kurt and Dimazzio are sitting outside your house right now in a dark blue Range Rover. Casares and Hoffman are just arriving, and they will stay inside and make sure she's safe."

I thought about it, then nodded. "OK, fine."

"Not at all, Harry. It's my pleasure. I do this kind of thing for all our operatives."

I sighed, telling myself I would never understand the Brits.

"Thank you, sir. I'll be there at noon."

I hung up and five minutes later the doorbell rang

and I opened to find Casares and Hoffman dressed like they were on their way to Florida to spend a week drinking beer and fishing. Hoffman, who was six three and had yellow hair on his arms, was wearing a straw hat, a blue shirt with red parrots on it, red Bermudas and Havaianas. Casares, who was half his size and black, had green Bermudas, a yellow string-sleeved vest with a green cannabis leaf on it and shades black enough to suck in galaxies and crush them to the size of electrons. He also wore a straw hat. They stepped over the threshold and Hoffman closed the door while Casares spoke.

"Just show us where the coffee is, dude. You go upstairs with your lady and get a couple of hours' sleep. Boss is gonna want you sharp when he talks to you, man."

I left them setting up a game of Trivial Pursuit and went up to Kate. She hadn't moved. I lay down next to her and slept for two and a half hours. Then I showered and dressed, took the Cobra and, vaguely aware that it was somehow ironic, drove to Flushing, in Queens, to meet the director of Cobra.

Maybe it wasn't ironic after all. Maybe I was just feeling ironic.

And bitter.

I found a space outside the Asian Jewel Seafood Restaurant, next door to the Hyatt, parked there and walked back to the hotel. The teenage boy in shirtsleeves at the reception desk pointed me in the direction of the cocktail lounge and I stepped in at precisely twelve noon. Brigadier Buddy Byrd was not there yet, so I leaned on the bar and ordered a double Macallan straight up. The kid behind the taps poured it, gave me a plate of peanuts and asked me how my day was going. I told him it was going OK. My great-aunt Mabel had just died in a freak harvesting accident and left me fifteen billion bucks and a ranch in Iowa. He told me that was nice and went to dry glasses where I couldn't talk to him.

Two minutes after that the brigadier walked in. He leaned across the bar and ordered a dry vodka martini.

"Shaken," he said, without batting an eyelid. "Not stirred." Then he turned and smiled at me without much warmth. "Shall we sit at a table?"

"Sure, why not?"

We moved to a small, beige circular table with small, semi-circular beige chairs. We sat and the barman brought over the brigadier's martini, with more peanuts. When he'd gone the brigadier looked me straight in the eye and said, "I have always considered you a friend, Harry. Even when you were in the Regiment. Whatever we decide today, I'd like it to be predicated on that friendship, rather than any kind of professional contract or duty."

"Yeah, I hope we can do that. I'm resigning, sir. My mind is made up."

"So I understand. And of course, if that is your decision, then I respect it and wish you well in the future."

He waited. I frowned, wondering why the hell he'd made me come to Queens just to tell me he accepted my resignation, and finally said, "Thank you."

He nodded once and said, "Now that we have established that, I have done you the courtesy of listening to you and accepting what you have to say. Will you do me the same courtesy?"

I sighed. It was a classic Buddy Byrd maneuver. He seemed to yield, then turned around and had you in a moral arm lock.

"Of course."

"We have two targets. They are major targets and time is of the essence. The job needs to be over and done with in the next four days. That is our window of opportunity. We may never get another one."

I shrugged. "Why me?"

"Because you are the only operative I have who will take on this kind of job, with virtually no intel or preparation, and pull it off."

I sagged back in my chair. "Jesus...! Is that supposed to be an inducement?"

"There are other inducements. We'll come to them in a bit. But right now I need you to understand how serious this is. And how serious the consequences will be if we don't do the job."

I picked up my glass, thought for a moment about putting it down again and walking out, but took a pull instead.

"Fine, tell me. I'll listen."

Have you ever heard of the Einstaat Group?"

I repressed another sigh. "Sure, if you surf the net it's full of them. They are the Illuminati, they are the Masons, they own the Federal Reserve, they control the world and they own the alien spacecraft that crashed at Roswell..."

He shook his head. "No, the US Air Force has that at an underground base near White Sands. The Einstaat Group is, if you will forgive the redundancy, *very* real. They meet every year at a different location, usually a very luxurious hotel, and the steering committee invites an eclectic group of billionaires, experts, academics, military brass..." He spread his hands. "In short, the people who shape the world—from Europe and North America. And there they discuss with each other their deepest concerns and aims for the world, free from the prying eyes and ears of the press."

"They actually *exist?*"

"Very much so. The steering committee is made up of two people. At present it is Professor Marcus Hoffstadder, possibly the finest economist on the planet at the moment, and Anne-Marie Karrión, a remarkable entrepreneur, married to a rather unremarkable billionaire. They have selected their guests for this year and the meeting, which lasts a week, gets underway today, in Andorra. The guests have been arriving over the last twenty-four hours."

"Who the hell are the guests?"

"Oh, in the past they have included such people as Prince Charles and Prince Philip, a number of US presidents, billionaires, innovators, academics.... There are about one hundred and thirty of them, and they are selected from the most eminent people in North America and Europe. Now, the thing is that since the '90s, the sectors of industry, economics, innovation and indeed philosophy have increasingly been represented by billionaires who have made their fortunes in the field of information technology. And they have also happened to be among the richest, most powerful men in the world. That tells you something about the nature of modern society, I think."

I grunted, felt a cold creeping sensation up my spine and reached for my whisky. He watched me a moment, then went on.

"For the last five years, according to *Forbes*, at least four of the ten most powerful people in the world have been William Hughes, Andrew Ashkenazi, Bob Zeff and Stephen Plant."

I said, "Silicon Valley: NanoWare, MyPal, Global Market and the SearchEngine."

He nodded. "Indeed, but we are not just talking about the four richest men in the world..." He leaned forward, raising his eyebrows high, "Though believe me, those four are by far the richest of the ten, by a very long chalk! Their combined net worth is well over half a trillion dollars. But we are not talking about wealth. What we are saying is that these four men, who are leaders of *private* enterprise within the field of IT, constitute half of the ten most powerful people on Earth. They are not heads of state, they are not kings or queens or politicians or generals. They are private citizens."

He paused to sip his drink and let that fact sink in. Then he added: "The other six are the presidents of China, USA, Russia, India, Germany and the UK."

"That's a sobering thought. But it's just a symptom of our age, sir. Two hundred years ago they would have owned coal mines, or shipping companies."

He stared at me for a long moment. "Yes, Harry," he said after a moment. "That is rather my point. You may recall how the Industrial Revolution played out. It started with the Napoleonic Wars and finished off in a grand finale with two world wars and climate change, and closing on nine billion people to enjoy the proceeds."

"OK, I take your point..."

"I'm not sure you do. That IT will define the next two hundred years is a given, but in what way is not so clear. You see, coal, steam, internal combustion—they all affect the body. But IT is *information* technology. It feeds directly into the mind. You have, I am sure, heard of AI, artificial intelligence."

"Of course."

"Have you heard of *hard* AI?"

I shook my head. "No."

"In a nutshell, hard AI says that thinking, in every form from feeling love or hate to compassion and self-awareness, is nothing more than very complex algorithms designed to trigger given responses. They tell us that it is just a matter of time before all computers become self-aware and start thinking for themselves."

"That's bullshit and science fiction."

He snorted. "I wish I could agree, but I would remind you that we have far outstripped *Star Trek* in all but space travel and teleportation. We are living in yesterday's sci-fi, Harry."

"Maybe so, but I still don't see what you're driving at, sir. So a lot of the world's most powerful men are geeks and nerds who were raised on Marvel comics and *Star Trek*. And once a year they meet to cut deals ..."

He sat back in his chair, shaking his head.

"No, Harry. That is not it. That's not it at all. Just be quiet and listen. Over the last few years it has become a growing concern of this small group of geeks and nerds, as you call them, that the world is becoming overpopulated. It was William Hughes who started the campaign several years ago, calling for involuntary sterilization in the most overcrowded nations. He is heavily concerned with climate change and its impact on the Third World, and though Ashkenazi and Plant don't trumpet it quite so much, they are also increasingly involved in researching clean energy, including fusion reactors. And in recent years they have aligned themselves with Hughes in expressing growing concern at the population problem, arguing that the greater the population, the greater the volume of waste and the greater the damage to the environment."

"So what are they going to do, sell virtual condoms?"

"Try not to be facetious, Harry."

"Maybe..." I was going to tell him to maybe get to the point, but I bit it back and said instead, "I'm still not seeing what you're getting at."

"Hughes, Ashkenazi and Plant believe that the World Wide Web, along with more than two billion computers that are connected to it, has obtained a complexity that allows it to achieve spontaneous AI: to in effect behave like a living, thinking entity, to make choices and take decisions for itself. The intelligence we have tells us that they intend to..." He paused, lost for words. "There is no term for it, Harry, because it has never been done before. The closest I can come is to say that they intend to release into the internet a cohesive program that will bring the entire thing together as a whole. For one purpose."

I was feeling kind of surreal. I asked, "What purpose?"

"It will sound quite innocuous when I first tell you, until you realize the uses it can be put to."

"So tell me."

"The idea is that the entire internet will be harnessed to control global markets."

I shook my head. "That doesn't sound innocuous. That means that whoever controls the software can cause booms and recessions at will."

"Oh yes, and a lot more than that. It can be used to trigger food shortages, famine, shortages of medicine, economic collapse. Essentially the software could be used to create artificial supply and demand channels that would favor the small group that owned and controlled it. So far as it goes, that is no more than a monopoly gone mad. But when you remember what those three men's main concern is these days, it becomes a little more worrying."

"Their main concern?"

He nodded. "Overpopulation."

FIVE

I signaled the waiter for two more drinks, then shook my head and told the brigadier, "No, I don't buy that an intelligent internet is going to cause recessions on such a scale that billions of people are going to die."

"No, I don't buy that either, and you are being deliberately facetious. Do you know why there hasn't been a war in Western Europe since the end of World War II?"

"Because the Germans finally got tired of getting beaten?"

"Because it hasn't been in anybody's economic interest. The exact B side of the reason that has had the Middle East in *constant* conflict over that same period. Governments go to war in order to accrue wealth and power, and it is market forces that dictate how and when that becomes viable." He shrugged. "Clearly it would not be economically viable for the European Union to march into Texas and claim the Texan oil fields, because in the ensuing conflict they would lose far more than they would gain. But in 1991, Saddam Hussein believed that it was economically viable to march into Kuwait. It was only a marginal miscalculation on his part. If he had waited for the Clinton administration he might have got away with it. Equally, the Bush administration estimated that it was financially viable to go into Kuwait to chase Saddam out. The point is, we have peace in the West, not because we have become more civilized, but because it is economically more expedient to conduct our wars abroad."

I frowned. "What's your point?"

"That this software allows the owner to engineer the economic and market conditions for wars wherever they are convenient. Huge benefits go to the financial institutions who provide the money for those wars, and to the military industrial complex who provide the weapons —and increasingly the software. And, at the same time, wars, big wars, are capable of decimating populations. Rwanda lost almost a quarter of its population in just a few months as a result of the war in 1994. The Congo had some thirty-four million people in 1990. Between 1996 and 2003 they lost almost six million people in two wars, back to back, almost a fifth of their population. And I am sure you are well aware of the statistics for the First and Second World Wars."

We were quiet for a while. Eventually I screwed up my face and shook my head at him. "Are you *sure* this can be done?"

"Of course, Harry, the personal fortunes of these men are like the budgets for small countries. But the money their companies move, the influence they wield over markets and public opinion is enormous. The sheer power they have even now is hard to fathom. And these men *believe* that human thought and consciousness is nothing more than algorithms. They have the technological know-how to tie not only all the significant markets on the globe, but the entire internet and web, into one, vast algorithm, with just two guiding principles:

A, benefit 'X' group of people—that's them, obviously—and B, trigger wars in Third World regions wherever and whenever possible, for the purpose of reducing world population. It could even control the supply of arms and ammunition."

I felt suddenly nauseated. "What kind of world are we living in, sir?" Even as I said it I knew it sounded naïve and childish. He smiled without much humor.

"When I was young, in the '60s and '70s, everyone was going on about the dawning of the Age of Aquarius, and how everything would be so much better. Well, old chap, welcome to the Age of Aquarius. Humans reduced to algorithms, and computers elevated to gods."

I looked around the bar, at the punters and the staff oblivious to us, oblivious to the insane, unreal conversation we were having, oblivious to the fact that they were an integral part of that growing web, that growing matrix that reduced them all to less than yes-no decisions on a monstrous flowchart. A woman at the bar in a turquoise dress laughed suddenly, and the sound was jarring and ugly. I noticed her cell on the bar beside her. I noticed for the first time the vast screen on the wall showing constant updates on the world news. A guy paying for some drinks at the bar handed over his card and the data from the card was fed into the till, which took his money and ordered another bottle of Beefeater Gin. No money changed hands.

"It's all one vast, computerized market," I said, half to myself.

He nodded. "Yes, that is what they have understood. But they have taken it one step further, and said that given one more, binding piece of software, it will become, in hard AI terms, a thinking market that can maximize gain for them, while simultaneously eliminating excess population."

"Who is it you want me to take out?"

"Those three: Hughes, Ashkenazi and Plant."

"But, in a sense they are right. It has already taken on a kind of life of its own. If they don't do it, their followers will."

He took a breath, as though he was going to say something, then paused before saying, "Let's cross each bridge as we come to it. They are not the only influential thinkers out there, Harry. We just need to stop them before they settle any agreements in Andorra."

"What about the software?"

"Any information you can get on that would be a bonus."

"When."

"Today. You fly to Madrid this evening, collect a car at Barajas airport and drive straight to Andorra."

"*Tonight?*"

"I have your papers with me, and all the information you'll need."

"Why the hell is this so last minute, sir? We need to do recon, preparation. The security at this meeting is going to be phenomenal!"

"No, phenomenal is the security each of these men has on their private estates. The security at Andorra will be tight and highly professional, but nothing compared to what any one of them has at home. And as to last minute, we found out yesterday that they were going to be there. It's the way the Einstaat Group operates, in total secrecy. Obviously they hope to catch any potential attackers or hostiles by surprise precisely so that they can't plan an attack in advance, but that very tactic may allow us to catch *them* by surprise." He smiled. "Nobody will be expecting the likes of you."

I drained my glass and set it down, licking my lips. "This is insane. This whole thing is nuts."

He leaned forward, intense and urgent.

"Maybe, but it's the only chance we get. We have a window of a few days, and we have to act swiftly and decisively. We can't let this go ahead, Harry, and I have no one who can pull it off other than you. You'll be back in a week —less. And if then you still want to leave, you can do so with my blessing, and our support and protection for as long as you both live."

He knew he had me. He also knew that his offer was an important one that would weigh with me. To have Cobra's protection for Kate, and for any kids we had in the future, was a big deal.

"What about hardware?"

"There's a hotel just outside Juberri, just across the border from Spain. You have a room booked there as Julian Ferrer. The owner of the hotel is a friend. You won't see him or talk to him. In a suit case in the wardrobe you will find everything we were able to imagine you might need."

I narrowed my eyes at him. "This is not a professional way to do a job, sir. This is not how we do things. I have no intel at all on the targets."

"I know, Harry. This is pure opportunism. The target has appeared and we are going to take a crack. Do the best you can. That is all I am asking. If you find it can't be done, abort. As simple as that. But give it a try, because if our information is right...it just doesn't bear thinking about the consequences."

I looked around the bar again and felt suddenly

oppressed.

"You have a car?"

"Outside."

"Let's walk and talk, or take a drive or something. I'm getting paranoid."

He paid the check and we stepped out into the noisy New York street. He had one of his dark blue Land Rovers parked behind the Cobra. I leaned on the roof and scanned the road up and down. Nothing caught my eye.

"OK, I'll do it. But there are conditions."

He crossed his arms and watched me, waiting. I said:

"I won't do it today. I'll go tomorrow. I spend tonight with Kate."

"You're being sentimental."

"No, I'm not. Somebody tried to kill me last night. Somebody who was being a damned sight more professional than we are being right now. They were trained for the job, armed for the job and knew where I was. I want to know who they were. Chances are even they'll try again. If they do, this time I'll only kill one of them. The other one's going to be singing arias. And that is relevant to the job because we do not want these bozos following me to Madrid and Andorra."

"Fair enough."

"Tomorrow you take Kate to a safe location, and you put a very discreet tail on me to see if I am followed."

He nodded. "Good."

"Finally, I take big spoils from Hughes, Ashkenazi and Plant. You'll need to facilitate secure transactions to a safe account."

He smiled. "We can do that. Anything else?"

I shook my head. "I'll let you know if anything

comes to mind."

He opened the door and leaned in to the backseat. He came out again with a black attaché case.

"Everything you need to know—your ID, papers, backstory, credit cards, instructions... It's all in there, plus the usual burners for emergency contact." He pulled the door open again and made to climb in. "Be safe, Harry. I may see you tomorrow."

He slammed the door and I watched him drive away.

I stood for a while after he'd gone, staring up and down the road, trying to sense if there was anybody watching me. I was pretty sure there wasn't, but I drove over most of Queens and Brooklyn for a good hour, going in circles and turning back on myself, before I finally headed back to Eastchester Bay, pretty confident that nobody was following me—and wondering why.

When I got there I told Kurt and Dimazzio, sitting outside in their dark blue Range Rover, that they could take the afternoon and the evening off. They told me I could go screw myself. I eventually persuaded them to call the brigadier. I don't know what he told them, but they packed up and left.

Inside, Casares and Hoffman were still playing Trivial Pursuit. I asked them if there had been any developments. Hoffman shrugged.

"We bin takin' it in turns to go up and check on her. Most 'as happened was she turned over. We checked last..." He looked at his watch. "Twenny minutes ago."

I gave a single nod.

"OK, so you can pack up your stuff. I'll take it from here."

"We should check with the boss."

"Check with whoever you like, guys." I smiled to show it wasn't personal. "Time to go home."

They made the call and ten minutes later they were gone.

I climbed the stairs, tapped on the door and opened it. She was awake, lying under the covers staring out of the window at the bay. She turned her head to look at me and almost managed a smile.

"Harry..."

I went in and sat on the edge of the bed. She reached for my hands and held my fingers lightly in hers.

"How are you feeling?"

"Doped."

"It will wear off soon."

"What happened, Harry? There's me mouthing off about being a Texan gal, and look at me, I needed to be tranquilized!" She smiled. "Some Texan gal, standin' by her man."

"Hey, it was a hell of a shock. It was my job for a long time, and I needed a couple of stiff ones, I can tell you." I hesitated. "I wasn't sure if you were..." I hesitated some more. "If you *were* going to stand by your man. No woman should be expected to have to put up with that kind of thing."

"Who were they?"

I gazed out of the window at the bay and hated myself for lying to her.

"It was a house invasion. This is New York. The Bronx! It happens."

"What did you do?"

I looked her straight in the eye. "I killed them, Kate."

She put her fingers to her mouth and I saw the

tears brim in her eyes. "What about the cops? Why haven't they arrested you?"

"Oh, the detective came, they knew the guys and they were satisfied it was a case of self-defense. He said it would be a waste of public money to prosecute."

She squeezed my hand. "Harry, don't lie to me. Who were the men you telephoned? You said..." She looked away from me, straining to remember. "You said you had two suits that had been ruined with tomato ketchup. You said the carpet had been ruined too. Then you told them you were with your girlfriend." She looked back at me. "Who were you talking to? You were asking somebody for help, Harry. I don't want the police knocking on the door in ten years' time..."

"Hey." I said it softly and placed my finger on her lips. "Take it easy. I called a friend last night. He's well connected. I told you my work was dangerous and involves very large sums of money. This guy is a kind of godfather. He watches my back. He pulled a few strings and there was no charge."

She smiled and squeezed my hand. "OK, but I wish you'd trust me. I don't like that there are secrets between us."

I inched closer and held her hand in both of mine.

"Kate, if you still want me, I spoke to my boss this morning and I told him I want out. He has agreed and he is going to give me a very generous payoff. But he has asked me to do one last job."

She frowned. "A last job? Where?"

"It will be just a few days, less than a week, then I'll be back and we can concentrate on us, on the ranch, on kids..."

She kissed my hand. "That's wonderful, Harry. I

hope this job isn't too dangerous. Do you have to go very far?"

"Not far. And I'll be right back in a few days."

"A few days? You think you'll be back by next weekend?"

"For sure, baby. By next weekend it will all be over. And listen, I've asked my pal to look after you while I'm gone."

She shook her head. "No, that's not necessary. I hate people fussing over me, Harry. You know that. I'll be fine." I could see her blue eyes growing heavy, as she was fighting the sleepiness. "I know... I'll tell you what I'm going to do. I'll go back to Texas, to my folks for the week."

I leaned over and kissed her.

"You don't worry about a thing. They'll take good care of you."

I checked the window, made sure it was closed tight, stepped quietly out of the room and went downstairs. I knew they were coming that night. I knew they were as short on time as we were. I also knew they were going to come in off the bay and up the beach. This time they were going to make sure they didn't underestimate me. So I had to be ready for them. Because I knew I was going to get just one chance. They were coming to kill me, or to interrogate me, which was worse. But I needed at least one of them alive, and that put me at a disadvantage.

A disadvantage I now intended to correct.

SIX

In a situation like this, I tend to remind myself of
the Lord's Prayer. My version. It says: Yea, though I
walk through the valley of the shadow of death, I shall
fear no evil, for I am the meanest son of a bitch in the
valley. And then I ask myself: "If I am the meanest son of
a bitch, and I was out to kill me, what would I do?" And
then I plan for that.

If I were out to kill me, in my house, I would send
three men, and I would send them in from the bay, up
over the sand, and I would send one to the front of the
house as a distraction, while the other two came in the
back.

That was what I would have done. And it was what
they did. But they didn't find what they expected.

I watched them through a night-vision scope from
my study upstairs. They arrived at two AM, disembarked
from a dinghy and crossed the beach at a run. They were
not carrying assault rifles, so they planned to keep it
quiet. There were four of them, not three, but one stayed
with the boat. The other three came to the narrow passage and steps that climb from the river to Shore Drive beside the Memorial Post. Two of them stopped and vaulted
the wall into my backyard. The third went to the front

door. It was what I would have done.

But now things started to go differently. I pulled on my night-vision goggles, vaulted the banisters and moved quickly into the living room, behind the front door. The front door which I had left open. I sensed him pause outside, a mere six feet from where I was waiting for him. I knew what he was thinking. He was thinking it was unexpected. The door should be closed. It didn't fit with their plan.

I heard the soft crackle of his mic, and his low murmur, asking for instructions. In the back garden, the two men had paused too. They didn't know they were being filmed by two night-vision cameras, and what they were saying was being recorded by high-sensitivity directional microphones. Now, one of two things would happen. Either they would tell this guy to proceed with the plan, or they would enter first, through the kitchen door, which I had directly in front of me. Normal operational procedure would be to go ahead with the plan. Because the open door could well be nothing more than an oversight.

A moment later the door eased a little further open. I remained motionless and controlled my breathing so it was shallow and slow. I heard him flip the switch a couple of times. Nothing happened because I had disconnected the fuse box. He took another step, and then another, so he was six inches away from me and no more than three inches in front of me. He had no goggles, which meant they planned to put on the lights. They thought they were going to take me by surprise, with superior force.

Which meant they intended to interrogate me. If they just meant to kill me, they would have come in with goggles, plugged me and left.

I heard him mutter, "I'm inside. Everything is quiet, but the lights don't work."

He never heard the reply. I reached with my left hand behind his head, smothered his mic and rammed the Fairbairn & Sykes home into the side of his neck, severing the carotid artery and the jugular veins. I gripped him tight, till he'd stopped twitching, then eased him down to the floor. I pulled off his balaclava, placed it under his neck and removed the knife. His heart had stopped pumping, so there was very little oozing, and what there was his mask caught.

I took his mic and moved through the black and green room, to the fluorescent green glow of the back door. I stood against the fridge, to the right of the door, and whispered into the mic.

"*Clear!*"

Two black shadows morphed against the green glow of the glass in the kitchen door. I had left it unlocked, and now saw the handle twitch and turn, the door opened and they entered.

They were nine feet away, with their left sides to me. I had the Maxim 9 in my hands. I put a 9mm slug through the nearest guy's head and splattered his brains all over his pal's face. They don't teach you that one at West Point or Sandhurst. You learn that one in the field.

He shied away and his hands responded to an autonomic reflex and went to his face. I had anticipated the position and put a second round through both his wrists. The third went to his left knee. It jerked violently, he made an incoherent noise and fell.

I took two steps, grabbed him by the scruff of his neck and dragged him so he was lying flat. He was spilling a lot of black blood over the luminous green floor. I pulled the mic from his ear and threw it across the room. Then I put one knee on his neck and pressed.

"Seems to me you're out of options, pal. You feel like talking?"

His answer was a rasp. *"Fuck you!"*

"Yeah? The way you planned this? The way you came in? I figure you've seen action in Iraq and Afghanistan, probably other places too. You're not a SEAL, you're not good enough, and you're sure as hell not Delta. But you're a pro. So you know how it goes from here on in. It only gets worse."

"Fuck you, asshole!"

"Keep going, soldier, and the best thing that can happen to you tonight is that you die, like your pals. Now, I'm offering you the chance to get out of here alive and with a pension. Who do you work for, and why are they interested in me?"

He had started convulsing as I finished my question. In that eerie green and black world I could see the foam spewing from his mouth. I swore violently under my breath. Whatever it was he had taken, it was going to kill him in minutes, and it was going to be a hellish death, probably by paralysis and asphyxia. I put a slug in the back of his skull, and put him out of his misery.

For a second I thought about going down to the beach and taking the guy in the dinghy in for questioning. But as I glanced at the microphone on the floor, beside the other corpse, I knew it was too late, and the distant, receding hum of an outboard motor confirmed that.

I checked the house and the perimeter while I called Cobra. It rang once and the same woman's voice said, "Please identify yourself."

"It's Dirty Harry again. I need the cleaning service."

I was fed through voice recognition and again there was a pause. "Where was the spillage?"

"My home. I have three suits stained with ketchup. The carpet's OK."

"Has anybody else been notified?"

"No."

"Are you sure?"

"Of course I'm sure!"

"Are you alone?"

"I'm with my girlfriend. She's asleep upstairs."

"I'm going to notify Buddy. There are two NYPD patrol cars headed your way. They have reports of gunfire."

"Shit! All the shots were suppressed!"

"It was a nine one one. I can't send the cleaners. Get off the line and destroy your phone."

I didn't have time to swear. I left the Maxim in the kitchen, pulled the SIM card from my cell and flushed it down the can. I still had the goggles on my head. I pulled the battery and put what was left of the phone in a shoebox with a powerful magnet that I keep for that purpose. Then I ran downstairs, snatched my regular, daily-use cell from a drawer and called nine one one.

"What is your emergency?"

I babbled, trying to sound like a guy who is trying not to sound hysterical. It wasn't so hard.

"I've had a home invasion! I think I have killed them..."

"Sir, are you calling from Shore Drive...?"

"Yes!" I gave her my address. "Please hurry! I think there might be more of them out there! My girlfriend is upstairs..."

"There are two patrol cars and a detective on their way, sir. You need to calm down. Can you calm down for me?"

"Yes, yes, of course…"

"I need you to lay down any weapons you have and step outside, unarmed, to wait for the officers, can you do that for me?"

I played along and told her sure, I could do that. I stepped out onto my front doorstep, holding only the cell phone, which she advised me to hang up and place on the floor, as the officers could mistake it for a weapon.

I hung up and slipped it in my back pocket, then stood on the front doorstep, listening to the wail of sirens growing louder as New York's finest came to the rescue.

This was a mess. It was an unholy mess, and no mistake.

They came from each end of Shore Drive, one from Layton Avenue, the other from Barkley, lights flashing and sirens wailing. In my mind I had the image of the guy I'd shot through the head, his microphone lying beside him. The last guy, the one in the dinghy, had heard the grunts, he'd tried to talk to them and they had not responded. So he'd called nine one one and got the hell out of Dodge. Whichever way you looked at it, it was an odd thing to do. It sure as hell wasn't the behavior of a criminal organization. If anything, it reeked of a government agent or officer in a real jamb, trying to save his colleagues.

They screeched to a halt, lying diagonally across the road outside my house, and climbed out drawing their weapons: two guys from the car on my left, mid thirties, athletic, nervous, one Latino, the other maybe Japanese or Korean. From the car on my right came an older guy, forty, with too many hamburgers and donuts under his belt. He was calmer, experienced, a sergeant with a moustache. Probably a family man. With him was a woman in her thirties, slightly overweight, long ponytail. The way she held her gun she was professional, but not experienced. She had never killed anyone, and was praying she wouldn't have to tonight.

That all passed through my mind in the time it took for them to brake and climb out, training their guns on me. I raised my hands.

"Relax," I said, loud but calm. "I'm unarmed, and I am the victim. This is my house."

A third car pulled up. It looked like a twenty-year-old Taurus, like the ones Mulder and Scully used to drive. A man climbed out of it who looked nothing like Fox Mulder. He was about five ten, with sandy, curly, uncombed hair going thin on top. He had three chins and a belly that didn't fit in his creased chinos. He shrugged into a beige jacket, and as he did it, one of his front shirttails came loose. He either didn't notice or he didn't care anymore. He walked toward me, chewing gum and holding up his badge, and breathing like it was a chore.

"Detective Mo Kowalski, NYPD. You call it in?"

"Yeah."

His small, pale blue eyes had gone to the night-vision goggles on my head. There had been no point in trying to conceal them.

"What's that on your head?"

"Night-vision goggles."

He gave a single, upward nod with his main chin, and his gaze went past my shoulder to try and pierce the darkness within the house.

"What's wrong with the lights?"

"I don't know. I think they took them out somehow."

His eyes narrowed and he scanned my face with care. "What's your name?"

"Harry Bauer."

"Got any papers that agree with you?"

"Sure, passport, driver's license, bills… They're all inside."

He chewed gum at me for a while, nodding, like he thought he'd caught me in a really bad lie.

"What else is inside, Mr. Bauer?"

I didn't hesitate. I looked him in the eye with no expression at all and said, "Three dead bodies."

He stopped chewing to stare at me, like staring that hard took too much concentration to chew at the same time. Eventually he started chewing again by slow degrees, first a down stroke, then an exaggerated ruminating circle, and then a close narrowing of his eyes. The product of all that intense focus was the question:

"Three dead bodies?"

"Yes sir. Two at the back door and one just inside here, at the front."

He took an aggressive step toward me and growled, "Git outta my way!"

I stepped to one side, and as he pushed through the door I said, "You'll need a flashlight." He stopped to scowl at me again and I reminded him, "The lights are out."

He turned and hollered over his shoulder, "Somebody find out what the hell is wrong with the lights! Get me the damn ME! And call for two meat wagons and the Crime Scene Team! *And get me a damn flashlight!*"

Within a second the sergeant with the moustache was on the radio to dispatch, the girl with the ponytail was handing Detective Kowalski a large, black flashlight and the two athletes were holstering their weapons and heading for the house at a run with their flashlights in their hands.

I stood in the door and watched Kowalski kneeling in the shadows, examining the body of the first guy, playing the beam of his flashlight slowly over the body, lingering over the hat I had wedged under his neck. He turned to stare at me and played the light over my face, making me squint and shield my eyes. The glare seemed to speak to me with Kowalski's voice.

"What did you do to him?"

I stabbed him in the neck."

"There's no blood."

"I didn't remove the blade till his heart had stopped. Can you move the light, please?"

It shifted and a voice called out from under the stairs, "Detective! The trip switch has been thrown! You wanna see it or should I put it back on?"

Detective Kowalski growled, "Nah, put it back on again."

There was a clunk and suddenly the ground floor was flooded with light. Detective Mo Kowalski was still scowling at me, the cop under the stairs was shielding his eyes, and his pal had wandered into the kitchen area, where the door stood open, and he was staring at the floor.

"Holy *shit!* Detective Kowalski, you really need to see this!"

Kowalski's eyes didn't stray from my face. He just said, "Come with, Mr. Bauer. Officer Ramirez seems to have found something remarkable. Maybe you can explain it to us."

I followed him across the floor to the kitchen. He took in the scene with a look of crazed wonder on his face.

He turned to face me yet again, shaking his head.

"You knew they were coming. You must have known. You killed the lights and put on your damned goggles. You took out number one by the door, with a knife. Then you waited in the kitchen till these guys come in. You took this guy with a single shot to the head. Then this guy..."

He frowned and hunkered down. "With this guy you suddenly go to pieces. What happened? You lost your nerve and started shitting yourself? You got him in the hand...no, in both wrists, in the leg...and then in the back of the head?" He peered down at his mouth. "And what's this, foam?"

He screwed up his face, like he'd wandered into Wonderland and was trying to interrogate the Mad Hatter. "A poisoned pill? Seriously? Son of a bitch! You didn't miss. You shot his weapon out of his hand and you shot his leg out from under him, because you wanted to interrogate him. But he popped a pill and you shot him in the back of the head. You executed him. You been playing war on my patch. What are you, Mossad? Whatever you are, you're in some *big* trouble, boy!"

I had nothing to say except, "I think I'd better call my lawyer."

He nodded. "I think you better had."

SEVEN

They'd taken me to the 45th Precinct, handcuffed in the back of a patrol car. Out of the rear window I'd seen them take Kate to another car. She was crying. The cops with her had seemed detached, uninvolved.

I knew they'd cross-examine her, and they'd make it tough, try to make her contradict my testimony. They'd lie to us both about what the other said and try to break our stories. My only consolation right then was that Kate had practically no story to tell. My cell phone was wiped clean, the SIM was destroyed, the attaché case was wrapped in plastic and buried in the sand at the foot of my backyard, and all the weapons I had at the house were registered.

They had processed us separately so we could not see each other or speak to each other, and then they had dumped me in an interrogation room and told me I could make one phone call.

I called the brigadier. It rang once and he answered.

"What have you done with the cell?"

"Wiped and disposed of. I need a lawyer and so does Kate. She needs one more than I do. I've been interrogated by tougher guys than these."

"They're on their way. We need you out of there within the hour and I need to know what the bloody hell happened tonight."

"Yeah," I said, laboring the irony. "So do I. I thought you were supposed to have this kind of thing covered."

"We are. Have you been involved in something privately? I need to know, Harry."

"Yeah, I've been trying to have a normal life and get married! No, sir, I have not been involved in anything privately!"

"Then this is a kickback from something prior..."

"There is something you need to know."

"What?"

"They were soldiers. They were dressed like special ops and they operated like special ops. The last guy bit a pill when I tried to question him. The detective has seen it and once the ME and the crime scene boys get a look, we are going to have one hell of a spotlight on us."

"We don't need this."

"Tell me about it."

The door opened and Detective Mo Kowalski stepped in and closed the door behind him. I ignored him and said, "When will our counsel be here?"

"They're on their way. They should be there soon."

"OK, I gotta go."

I hung up. Mo Kowalski sat opposite me and slapped a thick manila file on the table.

"Let me guess. You're gonna plead the fifth. You ain't gonna speak till your lawyer gets here. You're gonna wait for your influential friends to pull strings and get you outta this hole and outta here." He leaned forward, stabbing at me with his finger. "Well let me inform you of something, Mr. Harry Bauer, you had the bad misfortune to come up against a New York cop whose feet hurt, who suffers from acid reflux at night and can't get a decent night's sleep, whose wife screwed his best friend's wife and left him, who pays the kind of alimony only a lesbian judge would approve, and who has chronic backache. And worst of all, *I don't like you.* I don't like *anti-American punks* like you. So if you walk out of this station house tonight, it will be because you have cut my heart out with your Fairbairn & Sykes fighting knife, and bribed every damn judge in New York."

I jerked my head at the recorder on the table. "You want to repeat that with the recorder on?"

He shook his head. "No. This is just an informal chat between you and me, to help you to appreciate the seriousness of your situation. You know? I hate an awful lot of things, but one of the things I most hate, is a traitor. A man who joins a foreign army. A man who gives his loyalty to a foreign, enemy power."

"You're about three hundred years out of date, Detective. They've been our closest allies for a long time now."

"So why the SAS? Why not Delta or the SEALs? You didn't make the grade?"

I smiled. "I was in England, they offered me a job, I took it."

"That easy, huh?"

"Not really, no. Selection was tough, training was tough, but that was pretty much how it went down."

He leaned back in his chair and patted the file a couple of times with his open hand.

"So you were eight years in the British elite special ops regiment."

"One of them, yeah."

"So, basically, when it comes down to it, you're a trained killer."

"I'm a trained soldier, Detective."

He leaned forward and tried to skewer me with his small, piggy blue eyes.

"You're a trained killer, and you just killed three men in your house, using the skills you learned with the British Special Air Service."

"Is that a question, Detective?"

He turned and pointed to the door. I saw the sweat smudges along the collar of his jacket, and the large, damp patch under his arm.

"Any minute now, your counselor is going to walk through that door and start telling you not to talk to me. But one thing neither you nor he can get away from is that you, an American, trained by the British, killed what to me look like three American special ops soldiers on American soil."

"Is that something you can prove, Detective? Or is it just something you'd like to believe?"

"Nine tenths of it is hard fat, Bauer, and you know it. When the lab gets back to me, it will all be hard fat."

The door opened and Colonel Jane Harris walked in, in a smart blue suit with a white, ruffled blouse and a string of pearls around her neck. She carried a black attaché case and her legs looked nice in silk stockings. I was surprised that I was pleased to see her.

"Detective," she said, without sitting down and without looking at me, "I need to take my client with me right now. This is a military matter, neither you nor the New York Police Department have any jurisdiction here. Tonight's incident is a question of national security and falls within the remit of the Army."

He slammed his palm down on the table. *"Bullshit! That is bullshit! A triple murder was committed on my watch in my precinct, and you are not going to bullshit your way out of it!"*

She arched an eyebrow at him. "Shouting makes you louder, Detective Kowalski; it does not make you right or give you any more authority. You have no jurisdiction over this case or over my client. He leaves with me tonight and tomorrow a Military Police Investigator from the Provost Marshal General's office will be here to collect your report and any evidence gathered thus far, including, but not limited to, forensic evidence and oral or written testimony."

He struggled to his feet and pointed a fat finger at her. "You listen to me, lady…"

"Colonel!" It made him stop and falter. She didn't let him come back. "I have here a court order…"

She opened her case and handed him a slip of paper, which he read. His face flushed red and he scowled at her, waving the paper in her face. "I will appeal this! When my results come back, if those three boys were American soldiers, I will go after you and him and I will hold you both under the Patriot Act!"

She snapped her case shut. "If you did that, Detective, and if you were successful, which you would not be, the case would become a federal matter, and be handed over to the Bureau. In any case it is academic, because those results will come to me, not to you. Either way, I am taking my client now. You have your court order, you may try to appeal it, if you feel like wasting your time and taxpayers' money. I would recommend instead that you focus on a case that is actually within your jurisdiction."

He leaned across the table at me and stabbed his

ugly finger an inch from my face.

"I know you, Bauer. I got your face imprinted on my brain. I'm not going to let you go. I'm going to keep after you until I make you pay. You're a traitor to your country and a disgrace to your government."

I stood. "And you're a loudmouth, Detective. Take a cold shower, lose a hundred pounds of fat and you won't feel so bitter about everything. Have a salad for dinner."

"You just wait a minute!" He planted his hand square on my chest, snatched up the court order and stormed out of the room, snarling over his shoulder. "I'm gonna take this to the captain!"

The door slammed closed behind him and I glanced at the colonel.

"Is it legit?"

"Of course it is." But her eyes told me it wasn't. Not one hundred percent. The order was real and signed by the judge, but the case it purported to relate to did not exist. If the chief took it at face value, we'd be OK. If Kowalski decided to dig, we'd have trouble. She said, "Come on."

I opened the door for her and we stepped out. Across the busy detectives' room I saw Kowalski step out of his captain's office. Behind him I could see the captain, in his blue uniform, reading the order. He looked up from it and met my eye for a second. The colonel ignored them both and we walked out, into the small hours of the early Bronx dawn. The horizon was turning pale, and the green lamps beside the door cast a strange light on the windshields of the cop cars ranged in front of the old building. I stood on the sidewalk and watched her edge between the vehicles and walk to her dark blue Jeep. The lights flashed and bleeped and she opened the door. Then turned to look at me. Her eyebrows asked me if I was coming. I said:

"Now what?"

She shrugged. "Breakfast?"

"And then?"

"You really want to do this here, in front of the station house?"

I sighed. I felt tired. "What about Kate?"

"She's already on her way to a safe house. You coming, or are you going to stand there on the sidewalk till Mommy comes to get you?"

I moved between the cars, climbed in the passenger side and slammed the door. She got in, fired up the engine and the onboard computer told me to fasten my seat belt. I refused to obey until the incessant bleeping made her glare at me as we pulled onto the road.

"Your seat belt!"

"I know. I don't like being told what to do, especially by machines. Where is breakfast?"

"At the airport."

"Jeez!" I said quietly. "Buy a girl a drink!"

"There's no time for that. You have revised instructions and a new ID. You'll be flown by private jet to the *Aeroport Pirineus*, in Adrall, just ten miles from the border with Andorra, on the Spanish side. You have luggage in the trunk. Don't worry," she said with heavy sarcasm, "Buddy chose it, so it will be sufficiently rugged and male for you..."

"Still there, huh?"

She glanced at me. "What?"

"The chip. It's still there on your shoulder."

She dismissed me with a sigh and a slow blink. "You're Lou Hoffman, of New York. You are a software developer for Soft Games Inc. I bought you the *Idiot's Guide to Strong AI* so you can at least try to sound like you know what you're talking about."

"Wow, are we almost at the airport yet?"

"You have all your instructions, documents, et cetera in the attaché case, plus burners in case you have an emergency. Having said that, don't have an emergency. We can't afford another one. Weapons, you pick up as arranged. Don't talk to anyone, just collect the case and the bag from your room and go. Use latex gloves."

"Should I do my zipper up after I pee, too? How about my shoelaces?"

She swiveled her eyes to look at me. Streetlight and shadow washed over her face in a slow, steady rhythm against the paling sky outside.

"How about the three dead soldiers in your house, Harry? Shall we talk about them? What the hell were you thinking?"

"I was thinking, Jane, that somebody, a pro, wanted to kill me and I'd like to know who, and why *before* embarking on a job as important as this one."

"You should have informed us. We would have taken care of it and *you* should have left it until *after* the operation."

"Perhaps you should have explained that to them, before they came into my house to try and abduct and torture me."

She ignored my comment and plowed on. "Instead we are, once again, left cleaning up *your* almighty mess."

"Like the messes I left in Thailand and California? Get real, Colonel. You offer me last-minute jobs that are ill-prepared and ill-thought out, and you blame me for the mess. You know damn well that the five men who went after me wanted one thing. They wanted to know who I work for. And that means whoever *they* work for is watching me, looking for you. They are a threat to Cobra as much as they are a threat to me. I had to neutralize them, and I had to at least try to find out who sent them. Calling you in would have exposed you to possible discovery. That was not an option."

"You *should* have informed us!"

"And risk you telling me not to go after them?" I gave my head a small shake. "I don't think so."

She didn't answer. She kept her eyes on the long bridge ahead. We were crossing the black water of the East River, headed for La Guardia. Eventually she said:

"Your instructions are, go to Andorra, you are booked in at the Sport Hotel Hermitage. The Einstaat Group are meeting at the Grand Hotel, not far from you across the slopes. Locate and identify Hughes, Ashkenazi and Plant. Eliminate them. That's it. If you can gather intelligence on their proposed software, do so. But that is not a part of your brief."

"Got it."

"Where is the case you were given originally?"

"Buried at the foot of my backyard, in the far left-hand corner."

"Jesus Christ! We'll have to get it back tonight, and pray to God Kowalski doesn't find it!"

We came off the bridge and followed the Whitestone Expressway toward the airport. She said:

"Buddy tells me you're quitting."

"Yeah."

"For this girl, Kate."

"That's right. I figure if I don't get out now, and try and make a normal life, I never will."

She nodded. "I'm glad. The way you operate, sooner or later you'd get killed." She threw a sideways glance at me that had the ghost of a smile attached. "And that would be a shame. She's a lucky girl."

I stared out at the empty, passing roads, the houses and shops still shrouded in sleep and lingering dreams.

"Now I'm really worried," I said, and looked at her. She laughed and then we both laughed.

She left me drinking coffee and eating croissants in the VIP lounge, and examining the contents of the attaché case, while she went and organized my passage and my luggage. After twenty-five minutes she returned and said, "All right, soldier. Time to go."

I drained my cup, said, "Yes ma'am," with more than a touch of irony, and stood.   "Your cases are on the plane, they'll give you another breakfast on the way, and lunch and dinner. It's a seven-hour flight. If you don't flirt with the stewardess, you can get some study and planning in."

"Thanks for the advice, Colonel."

She nodded a few times and we stood in awkward silence for a moment. Then she said, "Try to come back, will you? I'll show you the way to the boarding gate."

She left me at the gate without saying goodbye, and I was led down a narrow passage by a pretty stewardess whom I had absolutely no desire to flirt with right then. There were no scans, no security, and I didn't have to take my boots off. I climbed straight onto the plane, strapped myself into a comfortable leather chair at a polished, oak table, and within ten minutes we were storming down the runway, headed for Spain, and Andorra.

I figured maybe this was how the point naught one percent lived.

EIGHT

I had touched down at seven PM. The day was still sunny and bright. I had got through customs and security without a hitch and found a rented, cream F-Type Jaguar V8 waiting for me at the airport. I guess the idea was I had to blend in with all the groovy, beautiful people who would be in Andorra that week. The cat had five hundred and fifty horsepower and an eight-speed transmission. But it was automatic, which took most of the fun out of driving it from the small, country airport, through the winding, forested mountain roads to the hotel in Andorra.

The hotel, when I got there, was Alpine in appearance, with a vast, sweeping wooden gable faced in huge sheets of plate glass. Inside, the lobby was all toffee marble, amber lamps and dark wood, and slim, smiling staff in dark blue blazers.

I gave the car keys to the valet and told reception to take my cases up to my room while I went for a walk in the gathering mountain dusk. The village of Soldeu was tiny, with six hotels, a handful of holiday apartments, a cable car and a narrow stream with a bridge. It was set at the foot of a deep ravine, with the sheer face of the *Coma Bella* behind it and the partially wooded ski slopes and the

Grandvalira Golf Course opposite, about a mile away or a little less. That was where the Grand Continental Hotel was, and where one hundred and thirty of the world's most powerful and influential men and women would be staying for the next five days.

That hotel was also Alpine in design, echoing the peaks of the mountains, but rather than being contained in one, single structure like the Sport Hermitage, it was composed of ultra-modern, concrete and glass cubes that sprawled halfway up the peak behind it. That peak, about five or six hundred yards above the reception building, was the only spot higher than the hotel itself.

An hour and a bit looking at satellite photographs on the plane had shown me that there were a couple of tracks through the pine forests that would take me almost to the top of that peak, and I wondered how many security guards they would have patrolling those woods at night. Could be none. Could be a dozen. I had no way of knowing. I knew if it was me, if I was in charge of security, I'd concentrate the bulk of my men around the building to make that impenetrable, and I'd have a couple of patrols in the woods as an early warning system. But that was just me. It was no guarantee that they would do that.

And to add to my misery, I had no idea what kind of hardware I would have at my disposal. The brigadier had said "everything we were able to imagine you might need," but anything I took from that would be just speculation until I got my hands on it.

My walk took me, by way of narrow, medieval passages among big stone houses, to the cable car which ferried passengers up to the golf course, and in winter up to the slopes. Right then there was a big sign on it saying, in Catalan and in English, that the cable car was out of service until the following week. So it surprised me to see a guy leaning against the doorjamb with a cigarette in his mouth, wearing what seemed to be a cable car attendant's uniform.

He watched me smile and climb the wooden steps to his porch with no real interest. I asked him, "You speak English?"

He shrugged and drew down the corners of his mouth. "More or less. More less than more, but OK."

"Why is the cable car suspended?"

He inhaled from his butt and watched it as he flicked ash.

"If no suspend, he fall down." He frowned at me, then smiled. "Is joke. Suspend. He mean hangin' on string. Same in Catalan and in English." He held his hand up in the air, like he was touching a cable. "Suspend," he said again.

I squeezed an expression of amusement onto my face and told him that was good and funny. Then I asked, "Why is it cancelled?"

"*Els Iluminati*," he said, and jerked his head toward the hotel across the valley. "They take the hotel, an' they throwin' the whole week there, talkin' about makin' war and makin' money. They doin' all kind of crazy stuff up there, bot nobody can doin' nothin' because they got police from Andorra, police from Spain, police from France, from Brussels, from USA... They got fockin' soldiers up there, protectin' these billionaire bastards. They doin' coke, drogs, orgies...."

He puffed his cheeks, blew out and shook his head, like he really wanted to be there.

"If only they'd invite you, right?"

He laughed. "I no like these people. You reporter?"

He didn't let me answer. "They don' like reporter. They don' let you write nothin'."

"Waste of time, huh?"

"My brother is a cop. They got every cop in Andorra up there. He toll me they bring in one hundred cops from France and from Spain, special anti-terrorist cops. They got CIA up there, with electronic surveillance. And they got a truck of special soldiers from France patrolling the forest. Like twenty special ops soldiers."

Five groups of four, ten groups of two, but French, so no real problem. I'd rather go up against twenty French special operatives than one Israeli trooper, any day of the week. My new pal was still talking.

"My brother, 'nother brother, he is editor of *Veu d'Andorra*, is newspaper. One CIA visit him, with chief of police, tellin' him, you no gonna publish nothing about this visit. You know? Everybody fuckin' here, most famous, most rich, but newspaper can say nothin'. This is the democracy? Bullshit!"

He spat to underscore that it was bullshit.

I left him staring at his cigarette and had a stroll around the town. The sun was down behind the peaks and dusk was closing in, but it wasn't night yet, and the glow of the streetlamps and the shop fronts was oddly bright against the blue sky. The streets were busy, too, with people doing last-minute shopping, or making their way to the bars and the restaurants which outnumbered the stores by two to one.

And as I walked I gradually became aware that this tiny town, this week, was like a who's who of all the people you never really notice in the news, unless you're watching and paying attention. Between the alley that led to the cable car, the Hotel Soldeu and the *Supermer-*

cat Font, I counted six billionaires with a combined personal fortune of over four hundred billion dollars. Four of them had made their fortune in the IT business. I also saw two world authorities on quantum physics, one on superstring theory, three astrophysicists and a renowned psychologist.

However strict they were being about not letting the riffraff get to the Grand Continental, the one hundred and thirty members of the world's elite were not being fussy about slumming it in the village. And that made me wonder who I might meet at the cocktail lounge at the Sport Hotel Hermitage.

I headed back at a leisurely stroll to find out.

The cocktail bar had become crowded since I had left to go on my walk. There were a lot of expensively dressed people standing in knots holding glasses, and they all seemed to be talking at the same time.

I did spot a financier whose family was reputed to partly own the Federal Reserve, and a British former prime minister who had opposed Brexit, but I was pretty sure these were not fifty percent of the world's most influential and powerful people drinking in the bar. I had a pretty strong hunch they might be their secretaries and PAs, though. I eased my way through the press and leaned my elbows on the bar. I ordered a dry martini and then turned to survey the crowd nearest me. There were ten, perhaps twelve of them loosely scattered. They were part of the same group, but they had fractured into small subgroups. I caught snatches here and there of what they were talking about. Mostly it seemed to be the quality of snow in the winter and comparisons of the food and the wine in France to the north and Spain to the south.

The barman delivered my martini and I took it for

a walk. That was when I saw the table in the corner. I made a point of not looking at them but instead touched a pretty young woman on the shoulder and smiled and said, "I'm sorry, have you seen John?"

She arched her eyebrows. "John Ashmore?"

"Yeah, Johnny." I moved my hand up and down as though to indicate his height. "Oh." She glanced around. "I think he went to the can..."

"OK, I'll hang around and see if I can catch him."

"Sure." She smiled and I moved off.

There is nothing more noticeable than the only person who's not talking to anybody in a crowded room. Conversely, those who are talking to each other become pretty much invisible. While I was talking to her, I had scanned the table with my peripheral vision and managed to glance at it twice. It was all I needed.

Ashkenazi was there, in the corner, with a potted palm on either side to keep him secluded from curious eyes. He was holding court with a bunch of his groupies and aides, wearing torn jeans, Nikes and a Harvard sweatshirt.

There were eight people sitting around him, hanging on his every word. Five guys and three girls. Most of them were in their twenties and early thirties, except for one guy with a tired suit and a big belly, who must have been in his fifties. He was sitting directly on Ashkenazi's left. On his right was a bald guy in Converse sneakers and jeans. His sweatshirt said Caltech and he kept pushing his glasses up his nose, like he was giving the older guy opposite him the finger. There were two other nerds slouched in their chairs. One was drinking Coke from a can, and the other was drinking water from a plastic bottle.

Next to the nervous guy with the finger there was a girl, about twenty-two, leaning forward with her elbows on her knees, holding a pad and a pen, and she was talking a lot directly to Ashkenazi. She was very blonde, with her hair in a ponytail and very pale blue eyes. She was also acutely aware that she was attractive. I couldn't hear what she was saying, but my imagination supplied a German accent.

Besides her, there were two other women. One was a serious forty-year-old in an expensive dress. She looked like she really wanted to be somewhere else, preferably somewhere with grown-ups who drank grown-up drinks. She was sitting next to the older guy with the belly and the suit. They were both drinking bourbon. Maybe it was a gesture.

The other was dark and pretty. She was drinking Aquarius and kept looking from the blond with the pad to Ashkenazi and then back again. She looked like she was anxious to please, and anxious to fit in.

I wondered where his bodyguards were. They should be easy to spot.

I stood by a potted palm and smiled and nodded at people who passed by, and eventually found two ex SEALs leaning up at the bar drinking water. They had spotted me but didn't seem real interested. I figured there was so much security around, they probably had me down as one of the European operatives. They probably knew everyone at the Grand Continental. But down in the town it was a different matter.

The dark girl stood and I heard the blonde say, "Oh, Melissa, can you get me one Diet Coke? You are zee doll!"

I smiled and made it to the bar ahead of her, and was leaning, waiting for the bartender as she approached.

I turned and smiled at her. She responded by glancing at me and pretending she hadn't noticed.

I said, "You don't remember me," which was perfectly true because we had never met before. She gave a small frown. "Sorry..."

She drew breath to speak to the barman but I cut in, "Aquarius, ice and lemon, and give me another Macallan, will you?" I turned back to her. "Meli..." I snapped my fingers several times in rapid succession, like I was trying to remember. "Melinda, *Melissa!* I'm Lou. Lou Hoffman! Don't tell me you don't remember!" She shook her head, squinted at me. I pressured her by laughing. "Come on! Don't break my heart! San Francisco..."

I snapped my fingers again, looking up at the ceiling. Suddenly she covered her mouth with her right hand. "Oh my god!" she said through her fingers. "Don't tell me you were at Comic-Con!"

I laughed. "I was trying to forget, but I saw you and it all came flooding back."

"Oh-my-*god!* Wasn't it the *worst?* Were you there? I *never* drink. I promise you, I *never* drink!"

"I believe you, but it was the only way to get through it and stay sane."

"I can't believe you were there!"

I goggled at her. "I can't believe you don't remember me! I thought we really connected. You hadn't had *that* much!"

"No." She frowned. "I think I kind of do now..." I watched her expectantly for a moment while she obligingly manufactured a few vague memories in order to make sense of the situation. People are skeptical about NLP, but it works. She narrowed her eyes and asked, "Were you with the guys from Twitter?"

"See? You do remember! Back then I was, yeah. So what are you doing here? Not much going on unless you come in winter."

"Oh, I'm like an assistant PA with Andy? Andrew? Ashkenazi?"

"Ashkenazi? Oh, *oh! That* Andy Ashkenazi! My! Well you are moving in exalted circles. Long way from the San Francisco Comic-Con, right?"

"Well, no! That's who I was with then. You would not believe how much inspiration he draws from art!"

"Art?"

"Yeah, comics and stuff! He is a real sensitive guy."

The waiter delivered our drinks and she leaned toward him breathlessly. "Oh, and a Diet Coke, please."

I made an effort to look shocked. "Oh, I'm sorry! Am I…? Are you with someone?"

"Yes! Well, I mean, no! Kind of…" She grinned. "I'm with…," she made little speech marks with her fingers, "'The Gang,' over in the corner." She held up the Coke. "This is for Anja."

"Oh, right, the gang." I nodded. "Is Andy Ashkenazi part of the gang?"

She leaned toward me. "He *is* the gang. He's like a latter-day prophet. My god! Wherever he goes he has a string of disciples following after him, hanging on his every word. He's, like, inspired or something." She stopped and frowned again suddenly, but blended in a warm smile with the frown. "I'm pretty sure I would have remembered you."

"Well," I smiled in a way I hoped was engaging, "I had hoped you would. It was a real nice surprise seeing you here, but I guess you're not used to drinking and a little goes a long way. Anyhow, I'll take what you said as a compliment."

She grinned and cocked her hip in a way that was charming and made me want to ravage her. "OK," she said, "you can do that."

She picked up her drink and her Diet Coke. I tried to look desolate. "Oh, are you…" I gestured toward where she was moving. "Are you working? Is this a kind of working evening…?"

She made a helpless gesture. "Well, you know, security? They don't really let us… I shouldn't really be talking to you."

"Oh, sure. No, I totally get that. Of course."

"You going to be around?" She glanced quickly over her shoulder through the crowd. I waited. She said, "I mean we're not really *working*, just kind of talking."

"I wouldn't want to get you into trouble…" My face lit up like I'd had an idea. "But, hey! Maybe if you're free for dinner, maybe later…?"

"Yeah?" Her face said she liked the idea. "I'll have to ask. You going to be around?" she repeated.

"Yeah." I grinned. "If there's a chance you'll have dinner with me, I'll be around."

She moved into the crowd, glanced back once to smile and made her way to the Ashkenazi table.

It had been a long shot, but it might get me some access to the groupie circle at least. I had a desperate lack of information about where my targets were located, and what their routines would be, and I had a maximum of twenty-four to forty-eight hours to gather as much intel as I possibly could. My only alternative was a ballistic missile strike on the hotel, and I didn't think the brigadier's case would stretch to that.

I popped a peanut in my mouth and made like I was

ignoring what was going on at the Ashkenazi table in the corner. It wasn't hard because not much did happen except that after a couple of minutes Ashkenazi spoke into his cell. A couple of minutes after that, the two SEALs at the other end of the bar moved and edged through the crowd toward me. I looked up and frowned at them as they took up positions to either side of me. One was black, the other was white, like the columns in Solomon's temple. Aside from that they were pretty much identical.

"Can I help," I asked them, "or is it chronic?"

"Mr. Ashkenazi would like you to join his table."

NINE

It was the one thing I had not expected, and it was the one thing I was not prepared for. But I guess that's what you get when you deal with dyslexic, dyspraxic nerds with huge IQs. You never know what the hell they're going to do next.

I was about to answer but didn't because I saw Melissa making her way back toward me with a big grin on her face. I smiled at my new friends.

"I think somebody is coming to get me."

The black one rumbled, "You'd better hope it's not one of us."

I nodded. "I do, fervently."

Melissa came up beside me and gripped my arm. She didn't even glance at the two monoliths standing beside me. I guess they were beneath her chat grade. "Andy says why don't you come and join us? And we can all have dinner together!"

She slipped her arm through mine and maneuvered me away. I grinned at the two SEALs. "See you later, guys, gotta go."

She guided me across the floor, sweetly and politely carving a path for us among the drinking, chatting nerd assistants. While we walked she squeezed my arm and whispered, "I think he wants to know what you're doing here."

That made two of us. It was a real temptation to look him in the eye, smile sweetly and tell him, "Well, actually, I came to kill you and your pals, Hughes and Plant," but right now I figured that wouldn't be smart.

The problem was, despite the colonel's thoughtful gift of the *Idiot's Guide to Strong AI*, I knew just about enough IT to write an email or search for Levi's on Amazon. So what *was* I doing there? Cobra had me down as a programmer, but I guess they hadn't thought that one through. I was going to have to think of something convincing, and I was going to have to think fast.

We arrived at the gathering and seven uninterested faces all looked up and watched me without curiosity. Not so Ashkenazi.

"You want to take my baby girl away from me?" He said it with a smiling mouth and unamused eyes.

"Given half a chance, that is what I aim to do."

His smile became bland, the most powerful man in the world speaking to a human insect. "Well, we can't allow that, can we? So why don't you join us instead? What's your name, friend?"

"I'm Lou Hoffman. What's yours?"

Everybody laughed except Ashkenazi. There was a touch of color in his cheeks. When the laughter died down he said, "I'm Andy." He made his way around the group, introducing each one of them, and finished up with, "...this is Anja Fenninger, my right arm, and this of course is Melissa, whom you met in San Francisco, at the Comic-Con, while she was under the influence of one too many margaritas. You'll have to tell us all about that. What a shame you didn't take pictures and post them on

Facebook." He looked me hard in the eye. "Somebody get Melissa's new friend a chair."

While one of his flunkies went to get me a chair, and they all shuffled and inched and edged to make room for me, he kept his eyes on mine and asked me, "So, what do you do, Lou? Let me guess, you're a computer programmer."

I laughed as I sat. "Not even close, Andy. I designed a staggered feed method for Sig Sauer magazines that was more efficient and reliable than the one they already had. I sold them the patent for a lot of money. They used it to make better guns and I took a couple of years out to tick a few things off my bucket list."

He didn't nod or anything. "You planning to kick the bucket soon?"

"I'm not in a hurry. You planning to help me? You designing an app?"

His smile was thin enough to model for Yves Saint Laurent. "No," he laughed, "that's Will Hughes's department. I'm just going to persuade people to use it."

"Right." I nodded, clicked my fingers and pointed at him. "Persuasion engineering. I was reading about that. How does that work? You install an algorithm in somebody's brain..."

He laughed. It was a mocking laugh and all his disciples laughed with him, though Melissa clung to my arm while she did it. "How do you install an algorithm in somebody's brain?" she asked.

I shrugged. "Isn't that the whole idea of strong AI? That the human mind is simply a matrix of extremely sophisticated algorithms?"

He raised an eyebrow and nodded once. I went on: "So you use some of the person's existing algorithms to form a new one: Do I want to be shot by a man in a black suit wearing a balaclava? No. Do men in black suits wearing balaclavas tend to hide behind doors in darkened rooms? Yes. Will I be able to avoid being shot if I turn on the light and look behind the door? Yes. Right? So automatically the brain installs the algorithm: Is the door open or closed? Closed. Is the light on or off? Off. So: Switch on the light and look behind the door." I offered a full-figure smile. "Bang."

He grunted. "Simplistic. We're not about changing the programming of people's brains. Bandler and Grinder started that whole game in the '70s. What we aim to do is improve on the existing models. The human mind is limited by two things. You know what they are?"

All his disciples looked at me curiously, to see if I'd get it right.

"You'd better tell me. I was pretty sure there were more than two."

He raised a long index finger. "Biology." A second finger went up. "A sense of 'I am.' Biology gives us emotions, among them fear, but also hope, faith, desire. All these things serve to filter out reality. It blows my mind..." He threw back his head and laughed out loud, forcing everyone else to laugh with him, even though they didn't know what they were laughing at. "All these New Age tree-huggers and angel worshipers want us to believe that the intellect is limited and we should go with feelings, which are far more spiritual. Yet intellect is the product of pure particles of potential, and feelings are the product of chemicals at work in our organs. How d'ya like them apples?"

He laughed again.

"So emotions confuse the algorithm," I said.

"Yes, and so does that sense of 'I' we are all so proud of. That sense of 'I,' that 'I am,' is like a massive gravitational force. It distorts everything, like a massive black hole in space. But AI is free of both those handicaps. AI can be engineered so that it has absolute awareness, without emotion, and disconnected from that artificial sense of 'Me.'"

"Huh!" I gave my head a little shake. "I thought the ultimate aim of AI was to create software with self-awareness."

He shook his head. "That's stupid. If they had egos, they'd not only be as confused as we are, they'd be in conflict with us. Asimov devised the basic laws by which robots would be governed in order to protect humans: A robot may not injure a human being or, through inaction, allow a human being to come to harm. A robot must obey orders given it by human beings except where such orders would conflict with the First Law. A robot must protect its own existence as long as such protection does not conflict with the First or Second Law.

"But personally, I believe wherever there is an ego, there is the potential for survival instinct, for pleasure and pain, wanting more of one and less of the other, and everything that follows from that: greed, envy, hatred, and ultimately rebellion and betrayal. Much simpler, much simpler—just don't give them egos."

I puffed out my cheeks and looked around the group. There was a hint of compassion in their smiles.

"That's all a bit deep for me, Andy. Philosophy never was my strong suit. But I have to say, I think you're going to have trouble making a machine think if it has no 'I' to think, 'I think,' or 'I wonder,' or, 'I'm going to do this, that and the other.'"

He pointed at me and shook his head. "You said it, Lou. You said the word right at the start. But see? Your mind is fogged by insecurities, preconceptions and emotions. The word, the magic word, Lou, is *algorithms*. Algorithms don't need the concept of 'I' or 'me' to work. The only reason nature endowed us with a sense of self was so that we would develop an instinct for survival. The 'I' must survive, right? But the need to survive brought with it fear, insecurity, and thoughts like, 'I don't want the man in black with the balaclava to be hiding behind the door. *So I am not going to open it! I am going to lie here with my eyes closed until he kills me!*'"

He had suddenly leaned forward and started shouting. Now he fell back in his chair and laughed out loud. He reminded me of a spoiled child scoring points off the people around him.

Melissa smiled at me kindly, like she was going to guide me toward the light. "Rational thought," she told me, "must be devoid of emotion."

Ashkenazi crossed one long leg over the other. "The Buddhists have been telling us that for two and a half thousand years. It's what meditation is all about, right? What are the two things that meditation seeks to achieve?" He turned to the older guy sitting next to him. "You don't meditate, Bob, do you?"

Bob shook his head. "No, Andy, I am too busy making you even richer."

"Yeah, but you might be even better at doing that if you meditated. Anja." He turned to the pretty blonde with the notepad. "What are the two things that meditation aims to achieve?"

He snapped his fingers. She said, "To still zee emotions ant lost zee ego."

He was circling around what the brigadier had been talking about, and I figured if I behaved like a fool, he might just keep lecturing me. I asked him:

"So, right, explain this to me. If you have no ego and no emotions, who gets to enjoy the results of all your smart thinking? I have an Aston Martin, a huge house with a pool, fifty billion bucks in the bank and a beautiful wife, but I have meditated so much I don't know who I am and I don't care anyway. Where's the fun in that?"

"You're missing the point, Lou, which is probably the reason why you don't have an Aston Martin and a hundred billion dollars in the bank, and I do."

"So what's the point I'm missing?"

"The software has no ego, so you can hang on to yours."

I made a big round O with my mouth and nodded. "Neat. That's cool, I have to admit." Then I frowned, like something had just struck me. "But, this is just, like, sci-fi speculation, right? I mean this kind of AI is still decades, maybe centuries away." They all stared at me without expression. "You can't actually make this stuff, right?"

Ashkenazi turned to the group. "This is why," he said, gesturing at me. Then he turned to me briefly and said, "Thank you, Lou. This is why," he repeated, turning back to the group, "it is so important to be in the hive. In the hive, information is shared, given to everybody, *disseminated!* This is what Plant understood: information *must be shared within the hive.* Because if you do *not* have the information, you *will* get left outside and you will be at the mercy of random, chaotic events."

He turned to me with his eyes narrowed, smiling and shaking his head. "But you don't even *want* to be in the hive, do you, Lou?"

"I don't know what you're talking about, Andy. But if it's called a hive, chances are I don't want to be in it. Isn't that where insects live?"

He pointed at me. "I know what you want, Lou. You probably want to be out, alone, in the wilds of Wyoming, hunting buck. Am I wrong? Go on, admit it. Am I wrong."

"You're not wrong, Andy."

"Instead," he said, as though he hadn't heard me, "of being here, witnessing the birth of a new age."

I chuckled. "Really? A new age? Or a New Order?" I raised a placatory hand, shaking my head and laughing. "I don't mean to be disrespectful, and, honestly, I think what you guys do is amazing. I am in awe, but a new age? When they built the steam engine—*that* was a new age. The Industrial Revolution. The British Empire, the Battle of Omdurman—that was the dawn of a new age. But allowing millennials, no offense, to share even more pouting selfies, or even more pictures of themselves doing things they think are," I made the speech marks sign and knew I had earned myself a special place in hell, "'crazy,' like standing with their arms and legs akimbo, or walking and laughing at the same time. That does not, for me, constitute a new age. Sorry."

There was a distinct chilling of the air. I felt Melissa draw away from me. Ashkenazi had that look on his face I had seen so many times in the past, when the big guy with his sleeves rolled up is about to lay into the guy tied to the chair, and break a few bones. He was smiling, but it wasn't the kind of smile that makes you feel warm and tingly.

"You're talking..." He turned to his disciples and gestured at me with an open hand. "He's talking about social media."

They laughed, like he'd said something funny. I smiled innocently and asked, like I was making a fool of him, "Aren't you, like, the king of social media? I thought you had pretty much single-handedly created social media." I paused, allowing my amusement to show on my face. "Which is an amazing thing. Don't get me wrong. Social media has changed the world. We have seen a lot more crazy cats than we would have, and God knows, spelling is being reformed, like it or not! I mean, who knew wanna and gonna were words, right? But wonderful as this is, new age? I don't think so. Trains, planes and automobiles, that is a new age. You know, the Battles of Santiago and Manila, the entire Spanish fleet virtually decimated in the Pacific and the Atlantic, by a few American vessels: end of an empire, birth of a new one." I leaned forward, looked excited. "In Santiago the American fleet outnumbered the Spanish, but the ships that took them apart were just a few, made of steel and with big, modern guns. And in Manila the American ships were heavily outnumbered, but they just sat there and picked the Spanish boats off, one after another. That was the beginning of a new age, especially for Spain."

He was quiet for a moment, watching me like he was calibrating me. "You always gravitate back to war and weapons, Lou?"

Melissa spoke reproachfully, before I could answer. "It's not all about war, Lou. There is nothing wrong in having fun together."

"Well." I took a pull on my whiskey. "Actually, most significant technological advances are made during war. War is a big motivator."

There was venom in his eyes when he answered me. I guess the tenth most powerful man in the world doesn't like being made to look small in front of his friends.

"Has it ever occurred to you, Lou, that maybe history is coming to an end? That technology no longer needs to evolve? That technology itself, in the form of the Web and its creators, has acquired a life and a motivation of its own? That would truly be a new age!"

I shook my head. "No. That's crazy."

He laughed noisily, mocking me. "Stick around, Lou! You are about to witness something extraordinary. You remember the panic of 1907?"

"I wasn't there, but I read about it."

"A small group of financiers were controlling the market by manipulating the supply of money in the US at that time. When they turned off the taps, and J. P. Morgan made a couple of choice comments to the press about how it would be smart to withdraw your cash from the banks in the face of what was coming, there was a panic run, and banks across America folded one after another. When it was over, Morgan and his pals swept the board and bought up all those failed banks. And then, John D. Rockefeller Jr.'s father-in-law, Nelson Aldrich, founded and chaired the commission that ultimately recommended the creation of the Federal Reserve, which was, to all intents and purposes, owned by J. P. Morgan, Rockefeller and their pals. And they're all here!" He laughed and pointed toward the door. "Not them, in person, they're dead! But their heirs. All right there, just across the slopes. Now..." He wagged a finger at me. "That, and the even bigger repeat performance in 1929, they were brilliant maneuvers, but imagine..."

His little group of acolytes had gone very quiet. He didn't seem to notice, and if he did he didn't seem to care. He went on: "Imagine if you had a computer the size of a planet, whose algorithms stretched across the entire global economy, and could trigger crashes like those constantly and at will, wherever it chose. But *always* aimed at benefiting those who owned the software."

I shrugged. "Sure, that would be a powerful tool, and it might render war unnecessary, but it's science fiction. It is much too complex to create for real."

He leaned forward and opened his mouth. Anja Fenninger, the blonde with the notepad, leaned forward and drew breath noisily, placing her hand on his knee. He threw her a venomous glance, but closed his mouth. To me he said, "Watch this space, warrior man."

He stood and his retinue stood too.

"We need to get back. We'll do dinner some other time."

Melissa gave me a sad look, like I had let her down badly, and I watched them leave. And shortly after that I watched the bar steadily drain of people. I wondered if I had achieved anything, and decided maybe I had.

I also decided I could not wait.

TEN

I had a light dinner of steak and salad, then had my car brought up and drove west and north out of town on the CG-2 toward el Tarter, and then bore steadily south, back toward the Spanish border.

The villages in Andorra are small and produce very small amounts of light. The mountains are big, abundant and heavily forested. They rise steeply from the few roads there are, and the result is, if you drive at night, even when there is a moon, you drive in extreme darkness, with vast black walls towering over you, blocking out the translucent sky.

The road wound on through Canillo and came eventually to the town of Andorra itself. I passed it on my right and plunged again into the profound blackness of the mountains until I came to the sprawling village of Sant Julia de Loria, with its tangle of twisting, winding roads.

I managed to negotiate them, among the nocturnal summer crowds that spilled from the sidewalks, and finally eased out onto the *Carretera de la Rabassa*, which zigzagged its way up through dense, black forest and then wound down into a broad valley of what seemed to be farmland. More endlessly winding roads brought me at last to the tiny village of Juberri, and just beyond it, set back from the road among pine trees, the hotel Coma Bella.

I pulled into the parking lot and climbed out of the car. The place was very still and quiet. Light flooded the stairs up to the main entrance, but made everything else seem even blacker by contrast. I crossed the lot and climbed the stairs to the porch. The door was open and I stepped inside.

There was a small, unoccupied reception desk on the right. Beyond it there was a space with a couch, a black leather armchair, a coffee table and a TV. Beyond that was a staircase that rose to the upper floors. There was no elevator. The TV was on and there was a man slouched in the armchair watching it, with his face resting on his left hand. I said, "Hi."

He looked up at me, but didn't say anything. I said, "I'm Julian Ferrer. I have a room booked..."

He used the same hand he was resting his face on to point at the reception desk. I looked and saw a key lying there, attached to a big wooden disk. The disk had the number 207 scorched into it. I showed it to the guy. He nodded and pointed at the ceiling. "*Segona planta, habitació set.*"

I didn't need to speak Spanish, or Catalan, to know he was telling me second floor, room seven. I crossed between him and the TV, making him shift his head, and climbed the stairs.

On the second floor there was a passage with three doors to either side and one at the end. The one at the end was number seven. I pulled on a pair of latex gloves, slipped the key in the lock and stood to one side, motionless, listening hard. There was nothing to hear so I turned the key and eased the door open. Nothing happened so I flipped on the light and stepped in and locked the door behind me.

The room was basic. A bathroom on the right, a short passage and a bedroom with a double bed, a wardrobe and a window with the drapes drawn closed. I left them that way, went and opened the wardrobe. There was nothing in it but a large suitcase and a large army kitbag, both of which I pulled out and dumped on the bed.

I unzipped the case and opened the lid. The brigadier hadn't exaggerated. I could have waged a one-man war to conquer Andorra, and won.

There was a pair of Sig Sauer P226 Tacops with extended magazines, my personal choice of gun. There was a Maxim 9 internally suppressed semiautomatic and the Fairbairn & Sykes was there too. Before doing anything else I strapped on the knife, checked and loaded one of the Sigs and slipped it in my waistband under my jacket.

There was an L96A1, probably the best sniper rifle in the world. It had been dismantled to fit in the case and, if I decided to use it, I'd have to put it together again. But that was easy to do. The rifle was designed to be adapted and even fixed in the field. There were a couple of cases of 7.62 NATO rounds to go with it, and as I inspected the weapon my mind went to the high ridge above the hotel.

There was a GVS-5 rangefinder, which might be useful, and a TAR-21 assault rifle, laser dot and night scope and plenty of ammo. In addition there was a sixty-five-pound, take-down Osage orange bow with twelve aluminum arrows, all in a drawstring canvas bag. And finally there were twenty-two pounds of C4, enough to do some very considerable damage, if put in the right place.

The kitbag made me laugh silently. It was the

NLAW: the Next Generation Antitank Weapon, designed by SAAB. It was light, only about twenty-five pounds, and though it was bulky, it was only three foot long, so easy to transport. Its only downside was that it was disposable. You use it once and dump it.

And that, aside from the night-vision goggles, was it. That was my arsenal. He had, as he had promised, provided me with almost everything he could imagine. And it wasn't hard to see what he had been imagining. He had foreseen that it was going to be very hard to get a bead on any of the three men, and like any good soldier he had come to the conclusion: if it gets too hard, throw a bomb at it.

The problem with that, was the collateral damage. There were a hell of a lot of people there, and I wasn't about to start massacring them just to get at my target. Having said that, what I *was* going to do was still something of a mystery.

I loaded the stuff up and carried it out to the car. The only sign the guy in the reception gave that he had seen me was to shift his head as I passed. I slung the kitbag in the trunk with some difficulty, as the F-Type is not big on space—I guess the idea is you send your luggage ahead in the Rolls with your butler—and put the case on the passenger seat beside me, then set off back to the hotel.

I drove down to the parking garage myself, left the NLAW in the trunk of the car and carried the case up to my room in the elevator. There I unpacked the whole lot, inspected it in detail, packed it back in the case—all but the bow—and slid it under the bed. Then I called down for a bottle of the Macallan and sat on my balcony, drinking whisky and looking up, across the valley, at the brilliantly lit Grand Continental, where a hundred and thirty of the world's most powerful men and women were dining, drinking wine at a thousand bucks a bottle, and discussing the destiny of almost eight billion people.

These were the new gods, the new Olympians, and if Ashkenazi was anything to go by, they were dangerously out of their minds. And what made them more dangerous now than they ever had been before was the fact that the technology they had at their disposal—the technology they were creating—was catching up with their manic dreams. Soon, they would be able to do the crazy things they fantasized about.

Soon, they wouldn't be fantasies anymore.

I reached for my laptop and the satellite photographs I had downloaded on the plane, started to leaf through them and to formulate a plan. In fact, it wasn't so much a plan as an exercise in sheer brutality.

At two AM I had made up my mind. I pulled on a dark sweater and the latex gloves, and stuffed a dark, woolen hat in my pocket. Then I took the bow and the aluminum arrows in the drawstring bag, dropped in the goggles and the twenty-two pounds of C4, and took the elevator back down to the parking garage. One thing I was very clear about: I was not going to get much sleep over the next couple of days.

I turned right out of the hotel and headed south for a mile and a half. There were still a lot of people out and about in the town, and more bars and restaurants than you'd think necessary for such a small place. But within fifteen or twenty seconds I was back in the pitch black of the countryside. And after a couple of minutes more I came to a track on the right which I had spotted earlier. I slowed, turned into it and killed the lights, then let the cat roll down the track to a large, stone barn. I eased it behind the building, out of sight of the road, and climbed out. I checked my fighting knife, my Sig and spare magazine, slung the canvas bag on my back and pulled the NLAW from the trunk. Then I vaulted the wall at the back of the barn and set off at a slow, steady jog across the fields toward the wooded slopes that led up to the golf course and the Grand Continental. I guess to a lot of people I might have seemed to be loaded down. But an SAS blade on an operation will routinely carry considerably more than I was carrying then.

After two hundred yards or so I came to a shallow stream. It was too broad to jump across, so I had to get my feet wet and wade across. I don't mind getting wet, but showing up at your five-star hotel at five or six in the morning with wet, muddy feet isn't a great idea if you're trying to keep a low profile.

From the river to the tree line it was another hundred and fifty yards over pretty even pasture, and I made that in a crouching dash. Once I was in among the trees I stopped and put on the goggles to set up the bow. Instantly the world turned to eerie green and black, and, with the bow set up and strung, I started to climb the slope. If there were guards posted around the hotel, then this was one of the places where they would be, patrolling, waiting, listening, patrolling some more.

It is not easy to move silently through a forest, especially if you're loaded down with a kit. But it isn't necessary, either. Every hunter, and that includes special ops operatives who hunt men, knows that a forest is full of noises that most people either don't notice or don't recognize. Forests come alive at night, but if you observe how wild animals move, you'll notice that their movements are sporadic, even jerky, and arrhythmic. Man is about the only animal that moves rhythmically, especially in a forest.

So, if you want to move undetected through woodland, you don't need to be silent—you need to be infinitely patient. You take one step, wait, listen, take another step, and only cover any significant distance when the ground is clear. I had a half-mile climb ahead, and I knew it was going to take me an hour at least.

I heard the first crack after ten minutes. I immediately hunkered down beside a large tree trunk, slowed my breathing and listened. There were soft rustles, another crack. The sounds were coming from ahead of me, farther up the slope. I wasn't familiar with the fauna of the Pyrenees, and I hadn't had time to look into it, but I figured they had deer, wolves and probably brown bears. The noises I was hearing suggested something large and heavy. It might be a bear, or it might be a man.

Then I saw a black shadow moving in the dark green light. It was hard to make out a shape. It shifted, blended with the trees and branches, disappeared and then suddenly emerged into a clearing thirty or forty feet away. It was the black silhouette of a man, six foot, broad, with an assault rifle slung around his shoulders. He stood very still for maybe ten seconds. I knew he was listening, and I knew he was listening for me. Then he signed his death warrant. He pressed a finger to his ear and muttered something. It sounded like, "Proceeding down the slope to check...," and that was when I saw his goggles.

If he was talking on the radio, his pal wasn't nearby, and if he was proceeding down the slope, and he had goggles, he was going to find me and alert his pal, and then there was no telling how many of these goons would come out of the woodwork.

So he had to die.

The arrow was already nocked and in one single, fluid movement I pulled back to my ear and loosed the barb. He heard the rustle of movement, because he stopped and stared in my direction. The arrow moved fast, at two hundred feet per second, and the razor-sharp broad head smacked through his sternum, cut through his heart and punched out the back of his chest, all in less than a quarter of a second. He didn't make a sound. He bled out fast and lay down on the dry pine needles to die.

I ran up to him and removed his earpiece. I fitted it to my ear and heard a voice saying, "Dave, are you receiving me? What's happening?"

I thought fast and whispered, "*We have an intruder.*"

"What's his status? Is he armed?"

"*No visible weapon, but he is moving up the slope. You'd better give me some backup.*"

He sounded skeptical. "Are you sure?"

"*Yes, goddammit!*"

He sighed audibly. "Just show him your weapon and he'll get the hell out of there."

"*Yeah, or not. Get your ass over here.*"

Another sigh. "OK, I'm on my way. You on the path?"

I looked up at where the dead guy had come from and saw that he had been standing on a kind of track or path. I smiled. "*Yeah. Hurry, will you!*"

I moved up to the track and knelt with my back to a large pine, in among some deep ferns. He took about three minutes to arrive. He was shorter and heavier than his partner, but he was light on his feet, and quiet. I let him get to twenty-five feet, then I noticed him falter and knew that he'd seen me, or thought he had. But by that time it was too late. There was the *thwack!* of the string and the arrow punched through his throat and broke his spine.

I went and checked him. He was about as dead as a guy can get.

"See?" I told him. "There *was* somebody climbing the slope."

I continued on up, taking it slow and careful, trying to decide how they had set it up. One thing was certain: sooner or later those two bozos would have to check in, and when they didn't there would be cops and soldiers swarming all over the hillside like ants.

I hastened my pace a little more and after another five or ten minutes the trees started to thin out. I advanced in short, crouching runs, from cover to cover, then dropped on my belly and began to crawl.

The road appeared fifty or sixty paces ahead of me, as a luminous, green ribbon running across an inky plateau. Beyond it the hill started to rise again, but now it was no longer covered in pines. It was largely bare, with shrubs, bushes and rocks. To the right I could see the golf links, and in the distance the green glow of the Grand Continental Hotel, sprawling up the side of the mountain, toward the bare peak.

To the left the road made a fork, a kind of intersection, with one branch running right, past the hotel and down toward the village of Soldeu, another running left into the woodlands and the third proceeding straight ahead from where I was lying. That one I figured led to the Grand Continental, because there was an improvised barrier across it and there were two guards standing at the barrier with automatic weapons.

I was under no illusion. These, like the two I had just killed, were peripheral, like scouts, keeping an eye on the outer perimeter. But once inside there would be no possible way to get close to the targets.

There are two ways to shoot a bow: with the arrow on the "inside," lying just above the knuckle of your index finger, or with the arrow on the "outside," lying just above your thumb. Most archers prefer the former, because it is easier, but if you are in a hurry and need to make multiple shots, you need to shoot from the outside, because that way it takes less than half a second to nock and draw. So I practice both.

Now I took two arrows. I nocked one and held the other hanging between my ring finger and my baby finger. I drew back to my ear, giving the bow its full sixty-five pounds and then some, aimed for the guard on the left and loosed. I didn't bother to watch and see if I hit him. I knew it would. I swung the second arrow up and trapped it with my thumb, pulled and aimed. A full second had passed and my first target was getting down on his knees, leaning forward as though to get on all fours. I could see a good five inches of the barb poking out of his back. His pal was just staring, uncomprehending. He didn't know what the hell had happened, but he was about to find out.

I loosed. A quarter of a second later the arrow thudded home through his ribs. Now he comprehended.

I sprinted across the flat, open ground of the plateau until I reached the slopes. Then I kept running at a steady pace, climbing through boulders and bushes, the need for caution now less than the need for speed.

It was almost a mile, running uphill. I keep in pretty good shape, and one thing you have to have in the Regiment is endurance. You learn that with the Fan

Dance, across the highest mountain in the Brecon Beacons, but even so, in the thin air of the Pyrenees and with the lack of sleep, by the time I reached the top I was exhausted. I dropped on my belly, rolled on my back and lay taking deep breaths, staring at the stars for a good couple of minutes. What I had was not a plan. There was no point in having a plan because there was no plan that would work.

What I had was sheer brutality.

ELEVEN

I left the NLAW concealed under some shrubs, slung the bow and the rucksack, with the twenty-two pounds of C4, over my shoulders and began a slow, sliding descent of the hill toward the sprawl of the hotel. I told myself repeatedly that this was an impossible place from which to mount an attack; and then I reminded myself repeatedly that everywhere here was an impossible place from which to mount an attack. And besides, there was no time for a rethink.

There was no time for anything. The clock was ticking, and their discovery of the dead guards must be imminent.

Slowly, out of the darkness of the night, sixty or seventy yards down the slope, I began to see what I had expected to see: the sheer wall that constituted the rear end of the hotel complex. It was staggered in height, because it was not a perimeter. This place had never been intended as a fortress. It was a luxury hotel in one of the countries with the lowest crime rates in the world. This staggered wall was simply all the connected back walls of the last and highest tier of suites and apartments in the hotel complex, which overlooked the streams, the cute wooden bridges, meandering lanes and gardens—it was the back walls of all the most expensive, luxurious suites and apartments in the hotel.

And there were guards, two of them, with dogs.

Luck played a part; not a big part, but it helped. What little breeze there was, was coming from the north-east, which put me upwind from the dogs. That allowed me to crawl slowly forward, inching over rocks and shrubs, until I was forty paces from the nearest guard, with his Doberman Pinscher. He wasn't doing anything. He was just standing, with his rifle hanging across his belly, peering out into the night, with the dog sitting at his side.

I had nine arrows left, and four targets. I made a rough estimate of how many paces I'd have to take to get from the nearest guard to his pal and decided he was forty to fifty yards away. Which placed him at sixty or seventy yards from me. That was too much. I had to close in and move to my left. Twenty yards would put all four of them in range.

Then the dog stood up—maybe he heard something, or smelled something, and his big head moved right across his master's lower belly. I didn't pause, think or hesitate. I drew two arrows, hung one as before from my ring finger, nocked the other, pulled and loosed, in one single fluid movement.

The razor-sharp broad head slammed through the wretched dog's brain and plunged deep into the guard's groin. Few things in life are as debilitating as damage to the groin area. The flow of blood there is massive and, by the time I had nocked the second arrow, half a second later, the guard and the dog had slumped to the ground.

I moved fast, letting gravity pull me, and covered fifteen yards in little more than seven seconds. But in a situation like that, seven seconds can be an eternity. I could hear the second guard, running, speaking French, saying, "*Bernard? Bernard? Ce que l'enfer faire? Réponds moi!*"

Which I figured meant something like, "What the hell, Bernard!" and meant that Bernard's pal was micro seconds from calling it in. If you shoot a bow a lot, the only way to shoot is intuitively. And the only way to shoot intuitively, is to shoot a lot. I shoot a lot, and in a whole variety of situations, but I always use the same kind of bow, at sixty-five pounds draw weight. It means I don't have to aim. My unconscious, or whatever it is, aims for me.

Bernard's pal helped me by running toward Bernard while he was swearing in Gallic, and so closed the gap between us. Even so, it was fifty paces in the dark with a moving target. I drew, right back to my ear to give the shot maximum power, and loosed the arrow. I aimed instinctively just a pace in front of him, and he ran right into the barb. It drove deep, dead center of his chest, tore through his sternum, his lungs and his heart, and punched out the back of his chest. Any ideas he had about calling in Bernard's death were shelved.

But his Doberman didn't quite see it that way. He ripped loose from his dead master's grip and came bounding up the hill toward me. It was a steep hill and as he approached he was forced to slow. He took my sixth arrow, at twenty yards, between his collarbones, straight into his heart. Death was instantaneous. I like to think he died the way a good Doberman would want to, trying to tear a man's throat out.

I scrambled the rest of the way down the slope, shaped my charges breathing hard but with steady hands, and placed them as strategically as I could. I stabbed in the detonator, synced it to my cell, and scrambled back up the two hundred or so yards to where I had left the NLAW. When I got there I collapsed. My legs were trembling with the exertion and my lungs were screaming for air.

I took ten seconds to lie on my back and do deep, rhythmic breathing, then I rolled on my belly and reached for the NLAW. I dragged it over, grabbed the range finder and focused on the front of the hotel.

I got a hot burn in my belly and a single, hot thud in my chest. There was a group of maybe forty or fifty men in uniform outside the front of the hotel. One of them was giving orders and shouting, pointing this way and that. There were four Wranglers and a couple of Range Rovers too. Men were scrambling, clambering into the vehicles, while others were arriving at a run from the building itself. I had seconds, if that.

I shouldered the NLAW and aimed. This superb weapon has two forms of delivery. It can drive its rocket straight through a wall or a fuselage and explode inside a vehicle or a building, or it can go overhead and explode above, raining fire and death on whatever is beneath it. The damage is massive.

That was the mode I selected now. I fired, watched the rocket leap from the launcher, ignite its engines, give a little buck and streak down toward the hotel. I had my cell ready when it arrived at the courtyard where the soldiers were assembled. I was a second out when I pressed nine on my phone, but the explosions were close enough to be practically simultaneous.

The rocket killed or maimed just about everyone in the courtyard. It detonated the gas in the gas tanks of the jeeps and the Range Rovers and created a massive fireball that engulfed the front of the hotel.

At practically the same instant, the plastic explosive went off. The C4 has a hell of a kick, but it is not spectacular. It's more like a really hard smack that lasts a fraction of a second and leaves a small cloud of dust, and total devastation.

I hoped, as I scrambled and bounded back down the slope toward the gaping hole in the wall beneath me, that I had achieved two objectives. The first was that when the head of security had raised the alarm because his boys' bodies had been found, all the guests, their secretaries and retinues, would have been confined to their rooms, or suites. That in turn would minimize the casualties, and help me to know where my targets were.

The second was that the big explosion at the front of the complex would concentrate what men they had left on that area, as the focus of an assumed attack, leaving a handful of personal bodyguards protecting their charges at the back of the complex, where the luxury suites were, and the big hole in the wall.

That was the plan, such as it was.

I scrambled through the rubble and the choking dust, ripping off my goggles as I went. I had been off by a couple of feet and the explosion had torn out the corner of an apartment, as well as blowing a hole directly onto one of those meandering paths. I knew, from the research I had done on the satellite images and the hotel's website, that the five most exclusive suites were on the left of the hole I had made, and now I turned that way.

There were small crowds of confused, dazed people spilling from the high-gabled, sprawling buildings, holding each other, weeping, staring, calling to each other. Here and there I saw guys with that unmistakable look of special forces, trying to herd the straggling people, ordering them to go back to their suites and rooms. Nobody was taking much notice. Everyone was in shock.

I sprinted. It was a cobbled path, seven or eight feet across, bordered by flowerbeds and decorative trees. It wound one way and another across the fronts of the most luxurious suites, past arbors, a wending stream and picturesque wooden bridges.

It was an educated guess, but an educated guess was the best I had. I knew where the presidents of China, Russia and the USA were, and they were not in Andorra. I also knew that the next in pecking order, in terms of power, included the three guys I was hunting. So two got you twenty that they would be occupying three of the five best suites.

Like I said, it was a guess, but an educated guess was what I had.

I ducked into an arbor that formed a passage to the Princess Suite, pulling my woolen hat over my face. I had made eyeholes so I could see and created a makeshift balaclava. I jumped up two wooden steps to the wooden porch and pulled the Maxim 9 from my belt. The door was closed, but somebody had seen me coming and wrenched it open.

He was big, six four at least, and built like an oak tree. Absently I registered that he was probably Samoan. His skin was dark and he was wearing white shorts and a white string-sleeved vest. He had a small disadvantage because he'd had to pull the door open, and that had telegraphed his presence to me. I double tapped and put two rounds in him. The first went through his right hand, tore two of his fingers off, knocked the Glock from his grip and punched through his chin. The second smacked a small hole between his eyes and tore out the back of his head.

He staggered a single step back and fell. I stepped over him with the Maxim held out in front of me. The room was big, ample, on two levels, with a glass wall at the back. A disembodied woman's voice was screaming, *"What the hell was that? Johnny! Johnny! What the hell was that?"*

Johnny might have been the Samoan lying on the floor, or he might have been the big blond who ran into the living room in his shorts, holding another Glock. The Maxim 9 spoke softly. It said, *Phut! Phut!* and broke his heart. He hit the wall and left a red streak on it as he went down.

I moved fast across the floor and into the short passage he'd emerged from. There was a bathroom and three bedrooms. The bathroom was empty and dark, one bedroom door was open and the bedside lamp was on. There was a single unmade bed. The second bedroom told the same story. The third bedroom door was closed.

I didn't pause. I kicked it in and trained the gun where I heard the shrill scream. There was a pretty young woman sitting in the bed. She was naked and her pink, silk nightgown was on the floor beside her. Next to her was a naked man, covering his head with his arms and begging, "Please don't kill me! Please! Just say what you want…"

I snapped, "Show me your face or I'll shoot you in the gut!"

He peered over his arms with weeping eyes and a loose, wet mouth. Steve Plant. I recognized him from the photographs I had seen. He was one of the five most powerful men in the world, and one of the three richest. Right then he didn't look the part.

I said, "Here's a simple algorithm, Steve: Is it Stephen Plant? Yes."

I shot him twice in the head and left. As I exited the suite I pulled off the woolen hat and stuffed it in my pocket. Then I ran. The crowds were thinning and most people were standing on their porches now, while their heads of security strode up and down in their underwear making phone calls.

I ducked into the second arbor, which led to the Emperor Suite, and saw two half-dressed security personnel guarding the door with HK 416s. One of them was a Latino quarterback with a tattoo on his shoulder. The other was a seasoned vet in his forties with a big, blond moustache. They advanced on me as I jumped up the steps like I owned the place. I snapped, "Colonel Jeremiah Jones! CIA! Where is Hughes?"

It happened in slow motion. The Latino quarterback glanced at his boss and for a fraction of a second his eyes went behind him, toward the door. The guy with the moustache hesitated, frowning, for a tenth of a second. He'd probably spent thirty years obeying orders. His brain registered the military attitude, tone of voice and rank. A tenth of a second was all the Maxim needed. One shot went straight through his heart and ended all his doubts. The second caught the quarterback in the eye and that was where his story ended.

Again I didn't pause. I blew out the lock and stormed right in with the Maxim held out in front of me. Again it was a large, spacious room on two levels, with a vast glass wall at the back. The furniture was modern and there was a copper fireplace in the middle of the floor.

William Hughes was in his dressing gown in the middle of the floor. He was afraid, but he was in control.

His wife was in the bedroom door, and she had a teenage girl with her. I snarled at the mother, "Get back in the bedroom, now!"

She stared at her husband. He looked at her and nodded. She left. I felt my finger tighten on the trigger, then snapped, "Come with me!"

He approached with terrified eyes. "What do you want?"

"Ashkenazi. I want Ashkenazi. Is he next door?"

"Yes."

"Take me to him. Now! Fast! *Run, goddammit!*"

I ran him out of the suite and along the wending path, maybe thirty feet or so. Then we ducked into a third arbor. We came out to a wooden porch, like the others, where two guards were standing with automatic rifles. The closest, a big blond with a radio jaw and blue eyes, saw Hughes and recognized him.

"Sir," he said, "you should stay in your suite until..."

I don't know what it does to your karma to die making an important statement that you never get to finish. I guess he found out. I shot him and his pal in the head. They hadn't hit the floor when I blew out the lock and kicked in the door.

Ashkenazi was there, but he was holding a revolver. It looked like a Smith & Wesson .44, chambered for a magnum round. He raised the gun and aimed it at my head. His hand was steady. He said, "Stay real still, Will. I got this."

TWELVE

If you are going to do surgical, precision work with a revolver, ideally you want a .22 caliber, or at least something below a .38, and a long barrel. The Smith & Wesson .44 is designed to kill grizzly bears and demolish small buildings. It is not designed to put a neat hole in somebody's head while not disturbing the coiffure of the woman standing next to him.

I took a small step behind Hughes, put my left arm around his throat and pressed the muzzle of the Maxim into the base of his spine. I smiled at Ashkenazi.

"I haven't got a lot of time. So I need to communicate with you fast and convincing. Do I need to kill or maim somebody in order to do that?" I waited. Neither of them spoke. I said, "Are there women in the bedroom?"

Hughes blurted, "No! No, you don't need to convince us! Andrew, for God's sake! Answer him!"

His answer was a mumble: "No, you don't need to do that."

I leered, "How about kids?"

"I said you don't need to do that!" He stretched out his arm, thrusting the revolver at me, like the gun would be more dangerous if he waved it around. "You must be out of your mind!" he said. "Do you think you can get away with this? How long do you think it will be before half of French and Spanish law enforcement and special forces are swarming all over this place?"

"Not long."

"You don't stand a chance!"

"I don't see it that way. Keep stalling and I'll blow your leg in half."

Hughes said, "What do you want?"

"That's more like it. I want the algorithm you plan to use to program wars and famine in the Third World."

Ashkenazi barked a laugh. "You *are* out of your mind! You fucking *are* out of your mind!"

I twitched my wrist. The muzzle of the Maxim poked out past Hughes's hip and I shot Ashkenazi through the right knee. He screamed like a parrot possessed by a banshee. His leg wobbled grotesquely, gushing blood, and he fell, gripping at his leg with both hands.

The bedroom door burst open and Anja Fenninger, the blonde with notebook, no longer holding her notebook, ran out screaming, "*Andy! Andy!*"

I kicked Hughes in the back of the knee. He fell on his face and I knelt on his neck, leveling the Maxim at Ashkenazi. The girl stopped dead in her tracks and screamed again. I said:

"Scream one more time and I'll shoot you in the mouth. Andy, the next round goes in your other knee. The one after that takes out your blonde friend here. How far do you want to take this? No time to design an algorithm. Make a decision."

He was whimpering so bad he couldn't talk. I looked at the girl and asked Andy Ashkenazi, "Does she know?"

He nodded, with his teeth gritted and his eyes

squeezed tight. He was sweating profusely and about to pass out. I said to the girl:

"You know what I'm talking about?"

Outside I could hear sirens. She swallowed and hesitated. I shot Ashkenazi in the other knee. He screamed with bulging eyes staring at the ceiling, the veins protruding in his neck. She screamed too and I leveled the gun at her.

"Do I need to kill him or do I need to shoot you?"

Hughes was smacking the floor with his palm. He said, "I can't breathe."

I said to the girl, "Time to make a decision. It's going to be an uncomfortable world for you, sister, if William Hughes and Andrew Ashkenazi both die because of your indecision."

She ran, back into the bedroom, and reemerged a moment later with a medium-sized rucksack into which she had stuffed two laptops and a bunch of other gear that looked like external drives. I grabbed it, slung it over my shoulder, stood and dragged Hughes to his feet.

The blonde was no slouch. She dropped easily to one knee, grabbed Ashkenazi's revolver and pointed it at me, holding it in two hands. I stepped behind Hughes again. I don't hit women or children, and I don't shoot them either. But I saw her eyes wince and her finger tense, and I knew that one round from that cannon could take both Hughes's head and mine. So I shot her, clean, between the eyes. She fell across Ashkenazi, covering his face and body. He didn't move.

Maybe I should have taken the extra time to finish off Ashkenazi. Maybe things would have gone differently if I had. But I was aware that time was running out, and every second counted. I figured he would bleed out in minutes, and I left. I shoved Hughes out on the porch. He kept saying, "Oh my God... Oh my God..."

I snarled at him, "He won't help you. Now run! I need you, but not desperately. Give me one small piece of trouble and I will kill you without a second thought. You believe me?"

"Yes," he said. "I believe you."

We ran back down the wending, cobbled path, between arbors and decorative trees. Over to our left two choppers were playing their spotlights on the courtyard outside the hotel lobby, while a third was making a search pattern over the golf links. Across the stream, seventy yards away, by the pool and the tennis courts, men in battle dress were fanning out, ordering people to return to their rooms.

We came to the big hole in the wall and I shoved Hughes through. "Climb," I snarled. "Your best chance of surviving to tell this on TV tomorrow is to do exactly as I tell you."

"I know," he said. "I understand that."

It was slow going, but we didn't need to climb the hill again. We only needed to find the cover of the sparse trees and the bushes, heading south and east toward the forest and the car. As we ran Hughes asked me, "What do you plan to do with me?"

"What you're asking is whether I plan to kill you."

"Yes, that's what I'm asking."

"I don't want to kill you if I don't have to. But you've seen that it doesn't take a lot to make me change my mind."

We had reached a ridge which was covered in pines. It was not dense forest, and you could see the translucent sky and the stars above, through the stenciled branches. Down the other side there was a steep slope, and back, to my left, I could see the choppers still focused on the building, though one of them had changed direction and was headed to the back of the complex. In a moment they would see the hole in the wall, and that would be a game changer. I snapped, "Come on!"

I dragged him to his feet and we ran hell-bent for leather down the steep slope. It was a bizarre image, a man in black holding a gun and a rucksack, and another in a dressing gown and bedroom slippers, running headlong down a steep mountain slope toward a black, impenetrable forest. He fell twice, struggled to his feet and kept running, until we fell suddenly in among the tall, whispering pines. Then he dropped to the ground on all fours, gasping and wheezing. He said three times, "I have...," and finally said, "I have to stop. I think I'm going to have a heart attack..."

I felt his pulse; it was fast but it was steady. I said, "No, you're not. Feel your pulse, with your fingers. Breathe in three beats, hold one, breathe out three, hold one. You got thirty seconds, then we move."

After twenty seconds he nodded.

"OK." He got to his feet and we began to descend the steep hill among the closely packed trees. "So, my original question stands," he asked, breathless, "What do you plan to do with me?"

"I plan to make a deal with you."

"What kind of deal?"

I glanced at him and snarled, "You do exactly as I say and I don't blow your arms and legs off and leave you here for the wolves and the bears."

He didn't answer for a moment, stumbling beside me, trying to keep up, but after a moment, he gasped, "All right, you convinced me you're a real badass and you have no compassion. That's fine. I've seen the proof and I believe you. But if I have to do whatever you say, what is it you say I have to do?"

"Shut up, and I'll tell you when I'm ready."

Five minutes later we emerged at the bottom of the slope, where the trees ended, and before us, lit now by a crescent moon, was the meadow I had crossed earlier; and threading its way through it was the stream, winking silver in the moonlight. There was no traffic on the road and the thud of the choppers was a distant echo, up among the peaks.

"Come on." I grabbed him by the scruff of his neck and we sprinted across the field, waded through the icy water and ran the fifty or sixty yards to clamber over the wall to the Jaguar. I shoved Hughes into the passenger seat, slammed the door and went round to get in behind the wheel.

"Now what?"

"Now we go to my hotel."

I fired up the powerful V8 but left the lights off. I reversed out from behind the barn and eased onto the blacktop. Moving at a steady forty miles per hour, pretty soon the town of Soldeu came into view. I switched on the lights, but nobody noticed us because, though there were dense crowds out on the streets, they were all staring across the gorge at the Grand Hotel, up on the ski slopes.

I nosed into the parking garage and killed the engine and the lights. We got out and I gave Hughes my woolen hat. "Put it on, pull it down low in case we meet anyone."

He did as I said. I grabbed the rucksack from the car and we went to the elevators.

At that time of the morning it was unlikely we would meet anyone, and right then everyone was either on their balcony or lining the streets, watching the fireworks up on the hill. So we made it to my floor and my room with no problems. I opened the door and shoved him in, closing it behind me. I pointed to the small desk where my laptop was plugged in.

"Sit. You want a drink?"

He moved toward the desk and sat. "Is this the condemned man's last drink?"

"I told you I don't want to kill you. You want a drink or not?"

"Sure."

I poured two generous measures of the Macallan and handed him one. He took it gratefully and I said, "Just press enter."

Then I wrote out two numbers on the hotel stationery.

"These are numbered accounts in Belize. You're going to transfer twenty million bucks to this one," I made a tick beside one of the numbers, "and you are going to transfer half of your personal fortune to this one."

I made a tick beside the other. His jaw actually sagged. He stared at me and his expression was one of utter incredulity, like he had seen the sun start to rise in the west. "You must be out of your mind," he said.

I gave a single nod and pulled the Fairbairn & Sykes from my boot. He stared at the knife in horror and held up both hands. I said, like I was telling him what time it was, or what the weather forecast was like, "I'm going to take off your baby finger on your left hand."

He scrambled backward and fell off his chair, sprawled on the floor, gibbering, "No, no, no...wait!"

I took a fistful of his robe, dragged him to his feet and dumped him back in the chair. "Listen, Hughes. I have not got the time to piss around with you. Do what I tell you to do and you might come out of this alive. One more procrastination and I will start taking bits off you. Now do it."

He started rattling at the keyboard, running his fingers through his hair, muttering, "I'm doing it, I'm doing it, but you don't understand. Twenty million won't raise any alarm bells, but you're talking about fifty billion dollars, I can't just... I'd have to make phone calls." He laughed like I was a moron. "I don't have a hundred billion dollars just sitting in my current account."

"How much?"

He was getting frantic. I was watching the screen and he was doing what I had told him. He spoke while he typed.

"There's maybe one or two billion in long-term treasury securities. Most of my money is in company stock. Then there are short-term bonds. I don't deal with this stuff."

I snarled, "Quit stalling!"

"*I don't know!*" he half screamed. "A hundred, two hundred million?"

"Whatever liquid funds you have. Do it now."

He sat and sweated and made the transfers while I pulled out one of the burners, leaned against the windowsill and called the brigadier. His voice was thick and sleepy.

"What?"

I looked at my watch. It was five thirty.

"Good morning."

"Is it done?"

"Partially. I have Hughes here with me..."

"Where is 'here.'"

"In my hotel room."

"Jesus Christ, Harry!"

"It's OK. I'm getting my spoils of war and he is kindly transferring a hundred mil into the company coffers. Andy very kindly gave me his software and I think Hughes might be able to help us understand it better."

He was silent for a long while. Outside the window, across the valley, I was watching a helicopter ambulance taking off from the Grand Continental. I figured Ashkenazi was in it, and wondered if he was dead or in a coma. The brigadier said, "What's your idea? Bring him to the airport at La Seu d'Urgell? We debrief him..."

"Sure, why not?"

His voice was hesitant. "And then what do we do with him?"

"Negotiate."

"I don't know why you can't just follow instructions."

"Give me some that make sense and I will."

"How does this make sense? What do we need him for?"

"You know as well as I do, if you're going into unfamiliar territory, you need a guide. You got anyone half as good as Hughes to guide you?"

"You're suggesting we could turn him and use him?"

"I can't think of a reason not to. Besides, he just gave you a hundred million bucks."

"Can you get him safely to La Seu d'Urgell?"

"Yes."

"Fine. Try it. Any problems, kill him. That *was*

what you were instructed to do. Take the CS 144 west to Civis, on the Spanish side. The border there is in the middle of the woods and there is no border post. Take the CS 600 from your hotel to Bixessarri. You get there via…"

"Sure. I know how to get there. I'll be at the rendez-vous in a couple of hours, maybe three."

"Your trust in yourself is as ever, awe inspiring."

I hung up. Hughes was watching me. He looked pale and sickly. I said, "I bought you a reprieve. We're going to Spain. I have strict instructions. If you give me any trouble I have to kill you."

"Who do you work for?"

"Don't ask stupid questions."

"Andorra will be crawling with cops."

"Not yet."

"How can you be so sure?"

I went to the wardrobe, pulled out some clothes and threw them at him. "Get dressed fast." I pulled out the attaché case the colonel had given me. I removed the false bottom and took out the fake ID I had for the return journey, which I had intended to make via France. I looked at the passport photograph, and the driver's license. In them I had very short hair, a moustache and glasses. She had kindly supplied the moustache and the glasses.

I tossed him the package and said, "Put on the moustache and use these glasses." He did as I said, in front of the bathroom mirror, and I compared him to the photographs. "You're lucky, you have a nondescript face. In poor light, we might just pull it off."

I tossed him the papers and his backstory. "You're Clive Andersen. Get familiar with your persona. Give me any trouble and I'll kill you *and* the cops. Believe me, you have only one way out of this."

He got dressed, I grabbed my luggage and we went back down to the parking garage. It was gloomy and the echoes of our footfalls sounded somehow dead and unreal. We climbed in the Jaguar and slammed the doors closed. Hughes said to me, "You were sent to kill me, and Andy. And to get the software Andy had developed."

I didn't say anything, but fired up the big engine and eased toward the exit. He said:

"But you didn't kill him, and you haven't killed me."

We pulled out into the gray dawn and I turned left and west.

"That's where you're wrong," I said. "If Andrew Ashkenazi isn't dead, he's as good as dead. And you are alive because I think you're useful." I gave him a smile that I was pretty sure he didn't enjoy. "Let's find out how useful you are," I said.

THIRTEEN

It didn't take long for us to get stopped. The crowds in the streets were gone, a pale gray light was beginning to illuminate the small mountain world, and high on the hill smoke and dust were trailing up into the sky, where helicopters were still circling, searching. On the main road out of Soldeu, at the first roundabout, the cops had set up a barrier. I didn't know if Ashkenazi had regained consciousness or not, but I was pretty sure at least a handful of people had overheard what had happened at Hughes's suite and at Ashkenazi's. So the cops would be searching for a single American male who had world-famous icon William Hughes as his prisoner.

As we approached the roundabout I handed Hughes my Wayfarers and said, "Put these on and smile a lot."

He gave me a look that said he was calculating the odds. I nodded.

"Fine, Hughes, let me explain. I have a Sig Sauer P226 under my arm. Alert this cop, and I will shoot you in the knee, then I'll shoot the cops, after that I will drive west and lose myself in the forest, dragging your stupid ass with me. Strapped to my right boot I have a Fairbairn & Sykes razor-sharp fighting knife. I will use it to cut your hamstrings and leave you for the wolves and the bears to eat, while I slip across the border and disappear."

By this time I was pulling up at the roundabout where a cop was telling me to stop. I smiled at Hughes.

"My advice, put the damn sunglasses on and smile."

He had the good sense to smile and nod, and put the shades on.

I had the soft top down and the cop came around to my door. I noted from his badge that he was a sergeant.

"English?"

I shook my head. "No, Americans."

"Passport!"

Hughes handed me the passport I had given him earlier. I added it to mine and passed them both to the cop. He glanced at them, frowned a moment at Hughes, and handed them back.

"Where you are staying?"

I pointed back toward the hotel. "At the Sport Hermitage. My friend is just visiting. What's going on? Last night, a bomb...?"

"You wait!"

He marched away and stood talking to another cop, gesturing at the hotel. That cop took our passports, got on a bike and roared off back toward the Sport Hermitage.

Hughes said, "If they rumble you, that won't be my fault. I have played my part."

I gave him the dead eye. "My instructions were to kill you. You're alive because I think you might be useful. Keep being useful, William, and you'll go home in one piece."

The cop with the charming manner was walking

back toward the car.

"Where you are going?"

Hughes answered for me. "We were going to have breakfast in Canilo, and then we were going to visit the church of Sant Romà de les Bons. And then lunch in Andorra la Vella."

His delivery was not affected at all, but he managed to make it sound vaguely gay. The cop's nostrils dilated slightly and he asked, "When you return to United States?"

I glanced at Hughes, "We thought maybe..."

"Early next week, we hadn't decided on a day. There is so much to see..."

The cop on the bike roared back, parked behind me and walked up to his chief. He handed him the passports and said something incomprehensible in Catalan, tapping Hughes's passport. I could feel the Sig heavy under my arm. There were the two by the door and another on the roundabout. But killing soldiers employed by people who plan massacres and genocide is one thing. Quite another is murdering cops who are just doing their job. I was going to have to let them take me in. But what about Hughes? Either I took him back, or I had to kill him. The sergeant was staring at me, without saying anything. Hughes was smiling like he'd been lobotomized. I decided, if the sergeant told me to get out of the car, I'd shoot Hughes as I did it.

The sergeant held out his hand. In it he had the two passports.

"You have a good day. Report to local police station tomorrow morning, and every day you are here, before twelve midday."

I took the passports like it was exactly what I had

expected him to say. He laid his hand on the door and danced his head around a bit, hunching his shoulders. "Lunch, no in Andorra la Vella. Before, in Encamp, you go to Hotel Paris. My cousin is own this hotel. There the food is good. You go there."

He patted the door and walked away, and we took off, nice and steady.

Hughes said, "I thought you were going to kill me."

"So did I."

We didn't talk again until we arrived at Canillo, about ten or fifteen minutes later. I was taking it easy because I didn't want to attract any attention. I was aware that the choppers were still scouring the area. I was real tempted to keep on going and get out of Andorra as fast as I could. But I knew that the cops in Andorra were talking to the cops in Spain and in France, and I wanted to make damn sure they weren't talking about Lou Hofstadter and Clive Andersen. So we stopped at the only café in town, Les Delicies del Jimmy, sat outside and had coffee and croissants while we watched the early morning drift by.

That was when Hughes started to open up. He sighed and dropped his croissant onto his plate, shook his head and said, "I just don't understand how you can do it. I am fully cognizant that I will probably die within the next twenty-four hours, but before I go, I want to understand *how* you can do this."

I felt, and fought down, a hot pellet of anger in my gut.

"Yeah? Maybe we can do a trade. I explain to you how I can do this, but first you explain to me how you can deploy a piece of software that will indiscriminately target Third World economies, plunge them into economic crises and provoke wars in which thousands, maybe millions will die, just so that you and your club of the world's most powerful men can clean up the profits."

He was shaking his head and got as far as, "That's..." But he got no further.

"Let me ask you something, Hughes: have you ever been in a war zone?"

"No."

"Have you ever walked into a small village where kids, children of four and five, are lying in the dirt in the streets, in their little short pants and pink dresses, with holes the size of grapefruits blown in them from machine-gun fire? Have you ever seen what we would call a toddler, clinging to its dead mother, caked in her blood?"

"I get your point. You don't need to..."

"Have you ever seen a child caked in mud, where the mud is made from blood and dirt?"

"No..."

I leaned forward. "Well that, Hughes, is just the surface of the horror. What goes on in a war zone is something that you cannot even imagine. Words like horror and despair stop having any meaning, because the reality is too much. But you..." I stabbed a finger across the table at him. "You are willing to inflict that horror on, not thousands, but *millions* of people, men, women, children, babies... For what? Because a personal fortune of one hundred billion dollars is not enough for you. You want more."

His voice was flat, without emotion. "You're wrong."

"I am? Because Andy Ashkenazi didn't seem to think so."

He sighed, shoved his glasses on his head and rubbed his eyes with the heels of his hands. "I can't believe this is happening. It's surreal."

"You think so, Hughes? Because the people you sentence to live in war zones, and the people you send out there to restore peace, find it all too normal."

He spoke, staring at the tabletop, deliberately, like he was biting each word off as he said it.

"You have got this completely wrong. Andy had an idea, a plan. We were *not* all a party to it. Some people were against it and some, like me, saw potential that could be drawn from it. But it was Andy's idea."

"Potential? You saw *potential* in plunging struggling countries into poverty and war to increase your own fortune?"

"No."

He picked up a croissant and tore it in half. I snapped. "Stop saying 'no' and explain!"

He looked at me under his brows and suddenly I saw that, nerd or not, he had the commitment to be a dangerous man. He said, quietly, "Stop putting words in my mouth, give me a chance to talk, and I will."

I slumped back in my chair, picked up my own croissant and tore it in half. He took a bite and sat back. I could see his hands were beginning to shake and realized absently that he was going into delayed shock. His voice was level.

"We are about to hit eight billion people on this planet. The population of the planet increases by about eighty million people every year. That is like adding a large European country to the planet every twelve months. People hear that and they think of overcrowding and resources. But it is much, much more complex than that."

"Complex? How? You arrange wars and genocides,

and you make a killing on your shares in ordnance and military IT. And you reduce population while you're at it."

He closed his eyes. "Will you please shut up and listen for just five minutes? The West—Western Europe, Britain, the USA—is to some extent overpopulated, particularly Britain and Europe, but the population is stable. Most of the increase is through immigration. But where population is ballooning is in Africa, India and Eastern Europe...in those societies where families traditionally have five, six and seven children, or more. But those societies have something else in common."

I dunked a piece of croissant and stuffed it in my mouth. "What?"

"The level of industrialization is low."

"So?"

He sighed, like he found my stupidity exhausting.

"It is an imperative of Western societies to feed, house and clothe the Third World..."

"You mean to sell to the Third World."

"That is irrelevant. Try and raise your sights a little higher, see beyond the obvious clichés. If the West amounts to one billion people, and China accounts for another billion, that leaves six billion people who to some extent do not benefit from post-industrial society. They are somewhere on the sliding scale of dying of starvation and living in a shack, to driving cars without onboard computers and having limited shopping options on the high street and online. They are economies that are largely rural and disposable income is low."

"What the hell are you getting at, Hughes?"

"The way the market works, East and West alike. It is the *imperative* of the market, not only that these extra people be fed, clothed and housed, but that they be given the immense, bewildering array of choices that we get crammed down our throats every day. They *must* get the latest computers, they must have access to Amazon, Twitter, Facebook, they must get credit to be able to buy all of this infinite array of goods, and not only that..." I waited, he stared at me and then spat out the words, *"They must have the freedom to create more industries to make more goods and sell them to more people!"*

"So what?"

"If this...," he stretched out his arm, gesturing at the world at large, "if *this* is what we have done by catering to two billion people, what the hell is the world going to look like when we industrialize to the point where we can produce and supply for *eight or nine* billion people?"

I sank back in my chair. He stared at me for a long time.

"Have you any idea," he said, "how much waste two billion people produce? Can you imagine the state of our world when we have eight or nine billion people producing full, Western-level waste?"

"No..." I said after a moment.

"India is already becoming one of the industrial heavyweights of the world. And there are more people in India than on the whole African continent. What happens when war and corruption come under control in Africa and they start building factories, making and marketing their own cars? Or when Ford, Dyson, Nike start opening factories there? What do we do with all the waste from production, the waste from distribution and the waste from consumption? *Four times* the waste we are producing already! Tell me, you, the judge, the jury and the executioner, what should we do?"

I stared up the morning street, where the shopkeepers were pulling up their roller blinds in the early light of the sun, greeting each other, pausing to chat and say good morning. They didn't look overcrowded, in this small, green mountain haven. They didn't look as though they were producing gargantuan amounts of waste. But I knew that was an illusion. Hughes was still talking.

"It's not just the greenhouse gasses, it's the plastics, the wrappings, the inconceivable quantities of *garbage* that a single city of six or seven million people can generate. Do you realize that New York produces more garbage than all of Norway? And that London and New York combined create more garbage than the whole of Scandinavia!"

"OK! I get your point."

"But I have to drive it home!" He leaned forward. "We are talking about two cities. Now add to that San Francisco, Mexico City, Sao Paulo, Rio, Paris, Madrid, Rome, Athens... on and on and on; and now add all the new, growing cities and new industrial nations, until you have not doubled, not tripled but *quadrupled* the output of *shit!* Even if we went nuclear and eliminated the CO_2, what about the toxic waste, chemicals, plastic, pseudo estrogens from the plastics, urine, excrement, and then all the extra industries created just to dispose of the waste! All, in turn, producing more waste. Your grandchildren will live to see this nightmare. Your children will live during the creation of this nightmare."

"OK!" I snapped. "But you cannot justify creating wars to cull the population, and while you're at it, line your own goddamn coffers!"

A few people turned and looked. He held my eye. "That was never my plan."

"Sure it wasn't."

"It wasn't. It wasn't my plan, it wasn't Plant's plan or Andrew's."

I planted a smile on the ironic side of my face. "Oh, Lord! Don't tell me it has all been some terrible misunderstanding."

"How many people did you kill last night?"

I didn't hesitate. "Twelve, thirteen if Ashkenazi dies."

"And you believe you had a right to do that."

I arched an eyebrow at him. "I believe it was a job that had to be done."

"How do you explain that?"

I folded my forearms on the table and leaned forward to speak very softly.

"Because there was this club of crazies who believed that they had the right to commit genocide and mass murder on a scale not imagined since World Wars One and Two and the Russian Revolution, and they thought that it would be neat to do it without ever getting their hands dirty, by creating the most sophisticated algorithm the world had ever seen, to manipulate world markets and create the conditions for financial collapse and war wherever it was deemed necessary. So, eliminating those crazies, so they wouldn't bring about yet another period of genocide and war, seemed to me to be a job that needed to be done."

He nodded. "Yes, I see that. But what *you* don't see is that what justifies the job for you is the simple fact that you don't like us. Because culling the population of the Earth is something that has to be done, one way or another, because the human species is a plague of parasites that will end up destroying its host. There are thousands of millions of people on this planet who consume resources and contribute exactly *nothing* in terms of wealth, culture, beauty, development. They are born, they consume, they receive handouts, and they die. And all along the way they generate waste." He barked a laugh and leaned back in his chair. "Do you know how many lives have been saved thanks to the technology I have created and facilitated with my software? *Millions!* Do you know how many doctors, scientists, writers, entrepreneurs, yoga teachers—*you name it—how many people* have become fulfilled and created wealth and happiness in this life thanks to the technologies that I created and facilitated? It must run into *hundreds* of millions. We have explored Mars and the solar system, we have stared into the heart of the cosmos, all thanks to what I made possible. And yet you feel you have the right to kill me, not because of what you think I want to do, but because you don't like me."

I stared at him a moment, wondering how much truth there was in what he was saying. Then I called for the check and said, "Come on, we have to go."

I stood and he sat looking back at me.

"You don't know," he said, "what we planned to do. But believe me when I tell you, it was at least as justified as what you have done and plan to do. The difference is your victims are privileged and easy to hate, whereas you see our victims as worthy and innocent. But the consequences for humanity, of your meddling, will be very far reaching."

The waitress came out, I gave her twenty euros and told her to keep the change. As she walked away with our plates I said to Hughes, "Shut up and get in the car."

He sighed and stood, and we made our way to the Jag.

FOURTEEN

W e continued on the CG2 and then, past Andorra la Vella, along the CG1 as far as Aixovall. There we came to a large roundabout where I turned left onto the CG6 and started winding up into the mountains, among dense pine forests. After about fifteen minutes we came to a small scattering of large, stone houses with gabled roofs, set to either side of a mountain stream. We passed a stone bridge and then the turnoff was on my left, the Carretera de Canòlich, the CS600.

It wound up steeply through thick forest, not just pines now, but oaks and planes, dense shrubs, ferns and brambles, a greenery that reminded me of New England just before the fall. We climbed for ten or fifteen minutes, and soon terraced orchards began to appear to left and right. Then there was a small esplanade, with a church and a restaurant, and after that we were climbing again, ever steeper, with a deep gorge falling away on our left, toward the top of the mountain.

We got there at ten AM, we crested the mountain and started to descend another winding road called, imaginatively, the Chicken's Depression. But at the first bend, almost concealed by the trees, there was the beginning of a broad dirt track that was lost in the shadows of the forest. I slowed and took the turn bumping and rolling at about five miles per hour. We were a hundred yards from the border with Spain. The only problem was, there was a large, black Audi SUV parked across the road. And there were two guys in suits leaning against the vehicle. Two guys I knew. They were Ashkenazi's black and white SEALs. The white one was holding a 9mm Uzi that would riddle us like a sieve if I tried to turn around and run. I figured they wouldn't want to hurt Hughes, but I didn't know that for sure, and I couldn't even be sure they knew Hughes was with me.

The white one strolled over, keeping the weapon trained on me. The black one came and leaned over my door.

"I told you once, you'd better pray I never come looking for you. Now I did, and you in some trouble, boy."

I jerked my thumb at Hughes, who had made no effort to move.

"You know who that is?"

"I know who it is. Nice moustache, Mr. Hughes. But right now," he said, turning his attention back to me, "I don't give a shit." He looked over at Hughes. "Mr. Hughes, we gonna get you back home just as soon as I finish breakin' this piece of shit into small pieces."

"Take your time, Paul. I'm in no hurry, and this should be interesting to watch."

It wasn't. It was all too brief. He swung a massive fist at me, as I knew he would. I weaved back and rammed the tip of the Fairbairn & Sykes into his wrist. It slid in easily and protruded out of the back. I twisted firmly, rammed open the door and stepped out, gripping his lapel as I did so, and slipping his Glock 19 from under his arm. I pressed it hard against his chest and fired four shots. The first two cleared a passage. The second two passed though that passage and smacked home into his pal's heart.

I turned and trained the Glock on Hughes. He was sitting passively watching me. "Was that interesting enough for you, Mr. Hughes?"

"You're quite something. Who do you work for? How much do they pay you?"

"As to who I work for, I could tell you, but then I'd have to kill you. As to how much I earn, this morning I made twenty million bucks. Help me arrange these bodies."

I took the Uzi and emptied fifteen rounds into the black guy's chest, making the original wound unrecognizable. Then I pressed the Glock back into his hand and put the Uzi in the white guy's hand. Finally, with Hughes's help, we positioned them so it looked like they had shot each other.

After that I went over the Jag with a cloth and removed any trace that I had ever been in it. Anything and everything that was mine or Hughes's, I transferred to the Audi, and everything of theirs I transferred to the Jag. The last thing I did was to swap the plates. I put the Jag's plates on the Audi, and the Audi's plates on the Jag.

Fifteen minutes had passed, and we drove, in the Audi, quietly and sedately out of Andorra and into Spain. Then it was a slow, meandering drive, skirting Andorra, through Civis, Asnurri and finally Argolell, small, stone villages set among green hills, forests and woodlands, until we finally arrived at la Farga de Moles, where I had, just a few hours previously, crossed the border into that principality.

Now we turned right and south, along the Spanish *Nacional 145*, and sped toward the airport Pirineus, just ten miles away.

The brigadier was waiting for us in the parking lot when we arrived. He was sitting in a cream Range Rover and climbed out as we parked. I almost didn't recognize him. He was wearing a pale cream suit with a bootlace tie and a white Stetson hat. His accent was believable, but made me frown.

"Mighty good of you to show, boy. But I thought you said a couple of hours."

"We were delayed," I said, trying to ignore his clothes and the way he was talking. "You know William Hughes...?"

"We've met."

Now it was Hughes's turn to frown. "We have?"

"You probably don't remember. You was busy talkin' about whales and savin' the Amazon jungle, or some such shit. I have a plane wait'n, if you'd care to follow me." Hughes drew breath but the brigadier cut him short. "Don't ask me mah name. That's somethin' you ain't never gonna know."

We followed him through the small, ultra-modern airport, through priority check-in and a private lounge and out onto the tarmac, where we boarded a Gulfstream V and sat ourselves down in luxurious leather seats while a pretty stewardess served us with martinis. Hughes had a Diet Coke.

Within a few minutes the plane had charged down the runway, lifted its nose into the air and banked east into a perfect, blue sky. I gave the brigadier a small frown.

He said, "We're going to Bar-see-lona." He nodded his head at me. "There, you're gonna have a frank and open discussion with Princess Lea and I am going to make sure that this time Mr. Hughes remembers my name."

Hughes's voice was level and steady.

"Are you going to torture me?"

"Fact is, as I am sure you know, Bill, torture ain't no darned use unless it's to satisfy the rage of the torturer. I feel no particular rage toward you, other than I think you're a darned fool, so I have no desire, nor need, to torture you."

Hughes drew breath to answer, but the brigadier just kept right on talking. I was beginning to enjoy his performance. I wasn't sure if he could fool a Texan, but he was sure fooling Hughes.

"What I aim to do with you, Bill, is clean y'up and get you back home as soon as possible. My intention, as I am sure you know, was to have you killed. You can thank Lou here for savin' your life. He thinks you can be helpful to us, and on reflection I'm inclined to agree. Course..." He sipped his martini and produced a smile that was unmistakably evil. "If you stop being useful, or play stupid games with your usefulness, well, I believe you've seen what Lou can do."

"How? How can I be useful?"

"Oh, in so many ways. First you and my boys are gonna have a long, open and frank conversation about algorithms. Then, we are going to talk about all the things that are most important to you in life, from your little puppy dogs, to your two lovely daughters—who I must say are most polite and accommodating—to your gorgeous wife. And then, when we have had that conversation, we are going to discuss exactly how somebody like you can help somebody like me."

Hughes opened his can of Coke and peered at it as though he might find that discussion inside the can and analyze it. "I might be able to understand that," he said, "If

I knew exactly who somebody like you was."

The brigadier laughed. "I am the mistake you never knew you made! You and your Einstaat friends were so sure you were the only cool kids in the playground, you were so sure that yours was the only show in town." He leaned forward and pointed a long finger at Hughes. "I'll tell you exactly what you and your IT pals thought. You thought, 'Information is power, and we are the Lords of Information Technology, so we are masters of the world.'" He sat back. "Now maybe you didn't think it in precisely those words, but that was the gist of it, am I wrong?"

Hughes shook his head. "No, you're not wrong."

"But you were, boy. Because information is not power. The fabric of the universe might be made of information, like Heisenberg said, but at the end of the day, all information does is *enable* power. Power comes from something very different."

He reached under his pale linen jacket and pulled out a Sig P320 and laid it on the table. He sipped his drink, smacked his lips and set it down.

"Take a step down from the abstract heights of your mind, Mr. Hughes, and you will see that even if the quantum particles that make up reality are indeed just tiny bits of information, you are not God and you do not know how to use that information. Algorithms are not enough. In human society power belongs to he who can deploy the greatest violence." He pointed at the pistol. "Power in this airplane belongs to the person who holds that pistol, and knows how to use it. Look at you, the most powerful men in the world, and one man was able to kill two of you and abduct the third. Why? Because he was the most violent. Violence, Mr. Hughes, is the source of power. It is the bottom line." He grinned. It was not a pretty grin. "And I am the single most violent man in the world. Do you know who I am now?"

Hughes nodded and smiled, and gazed out of the window. "Yes, I think I have some idea of who you are now."

The brigadier smiled at me. "The Einstaat Group, a lot of people equate it with the Illuminati or the Masons, shadowy groups like that. In reality it was founded shortly after the war, to strengthen Anglo-American relations, and to control Europe, which we had come to consider a bit of a loose cannon. Most of the people who founded it were Masons, of course, some of them very high-ranking Masons, and as it started drawing in visionaries like this crowd, and Elon, who had all been raised on *Star Trek*, they started bringing their crazy ideas and visions to the table. A colony on Mars, a world population brought into obedience by alpha rays or biochips..."

He threw back his head and roared with laughter. Hughes was watching him carefully. The brigadier went on.

"And now, strong AI. Now you want to unleash an algorithm..."

"It's not an algorithm. Stop saying that. It is more like a matrix of interconnected algorithms, very much like the neural circuits of the brain. But instead of being organic and carbon-based, this is silicon-based and does not need organic tissue. This is particle-based, information-based."

The brigadier growled, "Don't stop."

Hughes shrugged and shook his head. "We were going to feed it into the web and the net, and it was designed to grow into it, feeding on the information it gathered..."

"So it is AI."

"Yes, it learns as it grows, and it grows as it learns, attaching itself to all the streams of information that make up the World Wide Web, and the Internet. We called it the Overview Dynamic Intervention Nexus, mainly because Stephen Plant was obsessed with Vikings and wanted to call it Odin..."

"The god of war."

"Exactly. So, Odin would calibrate all the market information around the world, but not just markets, cultural dynamics too, historical tendencies, demographics, the impact of individuals like Trump, Johnson, Mercle—*all* the information that is available online—analyze it and act..."

I said, "Act? Act how?"

He studied my face a moment, as though he was wondering how I would react to what he was going to say.

"Whether you like it or not, Lou, there are too many people on this planet, and they are growing exponentially. We have no natural predators except...," he shrugged, "ourselves. We are going to destroy the planet and turn it into a hell. We decided we had to stop that from happening, and Andy came up with the idea of Odin. Odin would manage the global environment, physical and cultural, and bring about the conditions for war whenever and wherever it would benefit us, as an elite. That way, we would always remain in control. There would be no one to blame, but people would turn to us for a solution to repeated, constant war and poverty."

"So the people who would take the brunt of this brilliant idea were the Third World countries, condemned forever to poverty and the misery of war, so that..."

I trailed off because he was shaking his head. "No," he said. "That's not it at all. The next war, the one Odin was going to precipitate, was a world war, originally between Britain and Europe, with the USA supporting Britain, and China playing the part of Japan in the Second World War. It's a well-tried formula and it works. And...," he shrugged again, "a couple of nuclear strikes on China could erase millions, perhaps hundreds of millions, in one fell swoop, and liberate Tibet while we're at it."

I exploded, with a hot coal of anger burning in my gut. "*What damned right have you got, to decide...*"

But he turned on me and cut me dead. "Excuse me? *Excuse me?* You have just murdered a dozen men, *and* a woman, some of the most talented, brilliant people in the world, others just working Joes doing their job, and now you have kidnapped me and are threatening me with death and torture if I don't obey your instructions, and you shout at *me* about rights?" He stabbed a finger at me. "Even if you manage to salve your conscience and stop Odin, what is your solution for what is going to happen to humanity? How are you going to solve the massive overpopulation of this planet? Colonies on Mars, like that asshole Elon? Forced sterilization? And whom do we sterilize? Are we going to genetically improve the race by breeding out all the criminals? And how do we decide who is a criminal? Do we breed out the Marxes, the Engels, the Luther Kings? What about the Freuds? Do we breed out anyone who kicks against the state and authority? Have you *thought* about these questions? You're a killer! Perhaps we should breed you out! How many fine people have bad traits? How many intellectual giants revolutionized society? So how do we decide, Lou? You! You two are the great judges who decide who lives and who dies, not me! What I wanted to do, what we had planned to do, was simply to harness the natural tendencies of the market, and let the market decide. Leave it to an impartial piece of software, that would do no more than perpetuate what humans had been doing since the race began! Killing each other!" He stabbed a finger at his forehead, leaving an angry red mark. "What you brainwashed, conditioned morons cannot get into your simple skulls is that *humans need war!*"

FIFTEEN

We were met at Barcelona's interestingly named El Prat de Llobregat airport by two tough-looking customers in jeans and sweatshirts who looked as though they had just been recruited out of the Army. They called the brigadier sir, took his bags and led us through the airport and across the forecourt to where a Land Rover was waiting in the vast concrete parking lot, under the midday sun.

The two guys opened the trunk and threw the brigadier's bags in, then stood waiting. He held out his hand and said, "I believe you have something for me, Lou."

I nodded and handed him the laptops and the hard drives I'd taken from Ashkenazi. He turned to Hughes. "Get in, son," he said. And as Hughes got in the passenger seat, he added, "You'd better pray that what's on these computers is worth shit. If it ain't, you're in some deep trouble."

Hughes paused a moment, then slammed the door shut. I said to the brigadier, "You're leaving me here?"

"The last thing I said went as much for you, as for him. First you resign almost without notice. Then you were given a job, a job you could have accomplished and got away without causing trouble. Instead you decided

to spare one of the targets, another target you didn't finish, and you compromised the entire mission in order to
bring me this," he held up the bag, "and that." He jabbed
a thumb at Hughes. "I hope you realize how damned difficult it is going to be to turn that son of a bitch."

I was frowning. "You said Ashkenazi was dead."

"I implied it. You didn't confirm the kill."

"If I had left without taking the computers, the
whole mission would have been pointless. The software
was finished and only needed to be deployed. Anyone on
their teams could have deployed it. You know that, sir.
You need those computers, and you need an inside man
to help you understand them, and soon. Those people are
insane. They are out of their minds and are capable of
anything."

"You're preaching to the choir, Harry. You're not
telling me anything I don't know. But this was *not* the
mission you were given. If it pays off, you will have done a
superb job. Almost. If it doesn't, you will have screwed up
badly. Very badly."

"So what now?"

"I leave with Hughes. You wait here. Someone will
be along. You need to finish that job. I don't want to get
back to New York and find Ashkenazi in my office with a
letter of recommendation from you. I want him dead. Is
that clear?"

"Yes, sir."

"Good."

He turned and climbed into the Land Rover. His
door slammed and the truck took off. I stood, squinting
in the sun. That bastard Hughes had taken my sunglasses.
But as I shaded my eyes I saw, a hundred yards farther
down the line of cars, a bright red Ford Mustang GT. It

pulled out of a space and prowled up to where I was standing. The window slid down and Colonel Jane Harris looked up at me.

I smiled. "It's a girl, my lord, in a flatbed Ford, slowing down to take a look at me."

She didn't smile back. "Get in, Bauer. You really fucked up this time."

I slung what was left of my luggage in the trunk and climbed in next to her.

"It's nice to see you, too, Colonel."

She hit the gas and we powered out of the airport, straight onto the C32 freeway, headed north, back toward the Pyrenees and the border with France. She drove the way you'd expect her to drive, like she needed to prove that she could drive that way. When we were finally out of the city and cruising fast along the coast, with the brilliant green and turquoise Mediterranean on our right, she finally spoke.

"You didn't kill Ashkenazi. Do you understand that I am head of operations at Cobra?"

"No, I didn't know that. I have always dealt with the brigadier."

"Because he thinks you're special, and I don't know how to handle you."

I smiled. "Maybe he's right. But hey, Colonel, we're all special in our own way, right?"

She glanced at me and her face said she didn't think I was funny, but wondered if I did.

"You were given clear, precise instructions, Harry. Take out the targets, Plant, Hughes and Ashkenazi. Acquiring intelligence on what they were doing was only ever secondary. That was made very clear to you."

I sighed quietly and gazed out at the ocean that

was sweeping past. Far off a few brilliant white sails leaned away from the wind.

"I hope I am not boring you!"

"No."

You not only failed to take out two of the targets, you blew up a luxury hotel and *brought one of the targets back with you!*" She stared, incredulous, at the road ahead of her, spreading her hands on the wheel. "What the *hell* is wrong with you? Your orders were clear..."

I had suddenly had enough of her and raised my voice, not quite to a shout, but enough to shut her up.

"The orders were wrong!"

"I beg your pardon?"

"You heard me! The orders were wrong, and they were ill thought out! Yes, the targets needed to be taken out. But there were other issues that were not addressed. A, even if the targets were eliminated, the software could still be deployed, and because the software does not need a controller—it is true strong AI—then the damage would be done regardless of whether the developers lived or died."

She drew breath to speak but I plowed on without altering my voice.

"Shut up and listen. That meant that, B, the software had to be recovered so that at the very least our techs could analyze it and neutralize it. It also meant that C, we needed a man to help analyze it fast *and* operate on the inside at the Einstaat meetings to look out for our interests. Hughes was the obvious choice for that role."

Her face flushed and she glared at me. "That was not a decision for you!"

"No? Who was it for, then? Because you sure as hell hadn't covered that eventuality, and neither had the brigadier!"

"So now we have to run operations by you for you to approve them?"

"On the evidence, that would not be a bad idea. And you can be sure that if I keep seeing flaws in the operations, I will keep correcting them. Right now, instead of three dead geeks, you have one dead geek, the software you were so worried about, and an inside man in the Einstaat IT group. And as for the other geek, he's as good as dead."

"In that you are at least right, because by God you are going to finish that job!"

I looked at her and snarled, "You bet your pretty ass I am, Colonel!"

She glared at me. Her cheeks were still flushed red, but she didn't answer. I gave myself a private smile and asked, "What do you know about him? Where is he?"

"He's been taken to Paris for emergency surgery. Once he's stable he's being flown to New York."

"So get me to New York. I'll prepare for him there..."

"*No!*" She glared at me. "I don't know how the hell they ran things in the SAS, but in this outfit you *do not* plan operations and you *do* obey orders!" She drove in silence for a bit and then snapped, "Are we clear on that?"

I didn't bother answering her question. Instead I asked one of my own.

"So what's your plan? What do you want me to do?"

"We fly Perpignan Paris, we check in at the Paris Hilton as Mr. and Mrs. Brown..."

"You have got to be kidding."

"I am not kidding, soldier, and you'd better get that clear in your head. I am not Buddy and you will work the mission as I am giving it to you, or..."

"Or what? You fire me? I already quit, remember?"

She stared at me, but this time there was a glint of humor in her eyes.

"You'd better follow orders, soldier, or you will not be released. And don't think you can go crying to Buddy, because he is about as mad at you as I am. Who do you think dreamed up this cute little honeymoon?"

"Son of a bitch..."

I was quiet for a long while, as we climbed high into the mountains. The ocean glinted blue-green far below us now under the sun. Finally I said:

"I don't want to fight with you, and I sure as hell don't want to jeopardize this mission. We are agreed at least that Ashkenazi must be taken out. But..."

"You will obey orders, Bauer. There are no buts."

"Listen to me! I am good at what I do! If I weren't you'd have somebody else on this mission. Just listen to me."

"Fine, speak your mind, soldier."

"You have not got the experience, the field craft or the hands-on know-how to lead an operation of this type. You have to let me do this my way."

She didn't answer and we didn't speak again until after we had crossed the border, where she had handed over a couple of passports which the guard had glanced at and handed back before waving us on. It was only while he was doing that that I realized I still had the Sig in my waistband, and the fighting knife strapped to my boot. Once we were in France, descending toward Perpignan, she said:

"Right now there is no plan, because other than the fact that he is going to Paris, we know nothing. We are waiting on information. So, as of now, we go clothes shopping, attempt to make you look a little less like a hired killer and more like the refined husband of a successful, American businesswoman, and then fly to Paris and check in at the Hilton. So far does the plan sound OK, or do I lack field experience?"

"Colonel, I am trying to be reasonable. You can dress me up in furs and take me to the carnival if you want."

"Gee, thanks."

"But the planning and the execution of the hit…" I stared at her. She glanced back. I said, "That has to be my job."

She shook her head. "That may or may not be your job, Harry. We'll see when the time comes. But what *you* are going to learn on this job, is that you obey orders!"

"Why?"

She looked genuinely surprised. "What? *Why?* Because you're a soldier, Harry, and I am your commanding officer!"

I shook my head. "But I'm not a soldier. I resigned, remember? I resigned from the SAS and I resigned from Cobra. I am doing this as a favor for the brigadier. And once this job is done, I am out of here." We rode in silence again a little longer before I added, "And there is sweet FA that you can do about it."

She was real serious when she answered. "Toe the line, Harry. Don't make a mistake. You want to leave Cobra on good terms. Play nice." She glanced at me again. "Put your balls away and stop measuring your dick. We do it my way, and maybe, if you don't piss me off too much, my way will be letting you plan the hit."

I grunted, and after a while I said, "I need a beer, a

meal and a shower."

"You're not kidding, Mr. Brown."

"Jesus…"

"There's a place just outside Argeles-sur-Mer. They have cabins and a restaurant. I booked a room there. You can rest for a couple of hours, get some food. Meanwhile I'll go and buy you some luggage."

I stared at her sourly. "Are you the kind of woman who makes her husband wear pink shirts and sweaters?"

"I have never been married."

"Don't get deep, Colonel. Just don't buy me any pink clothes."

"Your name is Garret."

"Garret Brown?"

She nodded. "And my name is Sarah. You'd better get used to calling me that."

"OK, Colonel."

"You do it deliberately, don't you?"

"Yes, Sarah."

"I am an entrepreneur."

"And what do you *entreprendre*?"

She sighed. "What?"

"Entrepreneur is from the French, '*entreprendre*,' enterprise. It means an enterpriser, What enterprises do you undertake, Sarah?"

"I have a string of agencies, and we are in France seeking talent. Singers, actors, so forth."

"What about me? Am I a house husband?"

"No, you're a retired soldier."

"Retired, at my age?"

"Invalided out of the Marines."

She was starting to smile, having trouble concealing it. I shook my head, feeling suddenly like laughing.

"Go on then, I said, hit me with it. What happened to me in the Marines."

She raised an eyebrow and snorted. "You had your balls blown off in a freak accident. But don't worry." She winked at me. "I still love you, it hasn't really changed our relationship at all. Not even a little…"

"See? This is why they shouldn't let women into the Army. A guy would never do that."

She smiled the rest of the way to Argeles-sur-Mer.

It was like a holiday village, set back from the road down a drive among tall hedges, with a broad gravel forecourt in front of the reception, and then scattered cabins, each with its patch of lawn, set around a big swimming pool and tennis court. There was also a bar and a restaurant.

She parked and we went to check in. It took five minutes and her French proved to be fluent. As she signed and handed over our passports she kept smiling at me, and joking with the woman at the desk. When she was done we stepped outside again into the afternoon sunshine. She placed her left hand against my cheek and looked dreamily into my eyes.

"Don't get carried away, Harry. This is just me being thorough. I am a professional, you know. I didn't get to colonel just on my looks. I asked her if they'd make you a steak sandwich and give you a couple of beers. The kitchen's closed at this time. She said she'd do it herself. Isn't that nice?"

I returned her loving smile. "That's great," I said. Then I pulled her in close, took her face in my hands and kissed her long and deep. When I was done I bit her lip and whispered in her ear, "Ain't you glad we're sharing a room tonight?" Then I laughed boyishly and said, "Don't worry, sweetheart, I'm just acting too. Happy shopping, darling."

She climbed in the car and the pink flush in her cheeks had returned. As I watched her drive away I was pretty sure she was going to come back with half a dozen pink shirts, but I didn't really care. What was really playing on my mind, aside from the steak sandwich and the beer, was Ashkenazi, and how I was going to finish the job before he was flown to New York. Bombing the hospital, the airport and the airplane were out of the question. So it meant getting into the hospital and up to his bedside.

That would not be easy. But even as I thought it, an idea began to grow in my mind. The waitress, who was French and therefore cute, placed a large tankard of very cold beer in front of me, and in the kitchen I heard the hiss of steak on hot iron.

"To hell with Ashkenazi," I told myself, and the waitress smiled like I'd said something funny.

SIXTEEN

There were no pink shirts. There were a couple of expensive suits, half a dozen smart shirts, a couple of pairs of chinos, a couple of pairs of Levi's and some sweatshirts. There were also six pairs of socks and a couple of pairs of shoes, one black and one brown.

By the time I had showered and dressed, we had missed the flight to Paris. So we booked a room at the Novotel, by the river, in the heart of town and stayed the night. We could have driven to Paris and got there at twelve or one in the morning, by which time it would have been too late to do anything anyway. And I badly needed to rest. By waiting for the plane we could gather intel and still take action in the morning. The first flight got us in at eleven AM. By then we should know where he was.

The call came while we were boarding the plane. We were in the cramped aisle shoving our hand luggage in the compartments above the seats when her phone rang. I slammed the compartment shut and she slid into her seat, holding her cell to her ear. I sat next to her and she hung up.

"He's at the University Hospital Pitié Salpêtrière. He has had emergency surgery on both legs." She turned

to look at me and narrowed her eyes. "They have amputated them both from the knee down."

I gave a brief nod. "I figured. It's a shame they
didn't amputate from the knees up."

"You're a hard son of a bitch, aren't you, Harry?"

"What did you employ me for, Colonel? Did you
look at my resumé and think, 'Oh, here is a sensitive guy
who can engage despots and mass murderers in deep personal inquiry through the medium of dialogue?'"

"OK, Harry, he's a really bad man, but that is not
the whole story." She dropped to a hoarse whisper, "He is a
human being, and he has had *both his legs amputated*, because of what you did to him. Don't you feel *anything*?"

"Yeah. Regret that I didn't blow his brains out. If I
had, now I'd be on my way back to New York and retirement instead of being on this plane listening to this garbage. Skip it. How long is he in for and where does he go
from there?"

"You're unspeakable!" She stared out of the window a moment then turned to look at me again. "He will
be in Paris a couple of days minimum. Then he will be
flown to the Mayo in Rochester, Minnesota. Once he gets
there he is on his home turf and he will be much harder to
get to."

"It would be easier for you."

She frowned. "What? Me...?"

"Sure, you could pose as a counselor and talk him
to death."

"Enough, Bauer!"

"Then stop riding me, Colonel," I growled. "We all
know I'm a low-down piece of dirt who is only good for..."
She was staring at me hard and the next words came out
with a bitter twist as I looked into her eyes. "Who is only

good for the kind of work you farm out to me, because you can't bring yourself to do it yourself. I wanted to retire and you wouldn't let me. So get off my back and let me do my job the way I know best." I pulled out a magazine and started leafing through the pages. "After today, you can employ somebody more sensitive. Maybe a female reiki master."

"Jesus! You are so bitter!"

"It goes with the territory, Colonel. But then you wouldn't know that. Never having been to the territory."

"My name," she said in a voice that could have etched copper, "is Sarah!"

"And mine is Garret, darling."

She took a deep breath, puffed out her cheeks and blew. Then she said, "He's in a private ward, I'll give you the details when we get to Paris. Right now I really don't want to talk to you."

I didn't answer, and we spent the hour and a half of the flight in silence.

We touched down at Charles de Gaulle airport at five past eleven AM and the colonel went to collect the car she'd hired with the flight. It was a French car, and while she was signing the papers I said, "I need you to drop me at a fancy dress store."

She raised an eyebrow without looking up from the papers.

"You finally found your calling?"

"I need a doctor's gown, a beard and moustache and some glasses."

She picked up the keys and we started walking toward the car depots. "Then what you need," she said, "is a medical supplies shop. There's one on Rue Monsieur le Prince!"

"You happen to know that?"

We stepped into an elevator and started down toward the lower levels of the parking garage. She gave me an inscrutable smile that lasted a little too long and finally said, "You're not the first man in Paris that I have dressed up as a doctor, Garret."

"Oh. Perhaps we should get a nurse's uniform while we're at it, then. Or, as we're in Paris, a French maid's uniform."

"Quit while you're ahead, boy."

"Just going with the flow, Sarah. I also need a moustache and some glasses. Can we get them at the medical supply store too?"

We made our way through the late-morning Paris traffic, which is only a little more stressful than a war zone, and eventually came to park outside a cocktail bar and a foot massage parlor. The medical supplies shop was a short walk up the street, and all the way there we continued without talking to each other, which suited me fine.

I bought a stethoscope, a white lab coat and a pen that was also a flashlight, for looking down people's throats. The colonel watched me with amused disdain and when we'd finished and she'd paid, she told me, as we stepped back into the street, "You know doctors don't dress like that anymore."

"Really? I wouldn't know. I never go to hospitals unless it's to kill somebody."

She ignored me and went on. "They wear baggy green things, and clogs."

"I'm not that kind of doctor. I'm the kind of doctor I used to watch on TV. They had gravitas and inspired respect. How can you get better, if your doctor is dressed like an orderly?"

We stopped by the car. She said, "So now what?"

"I need some glasses, and a moustache and a beard. After that, drop me one street from the hospital. I'll walk the rest of the way. I'll call you from the burner when I'm done."

She nodded. She wasn't smiling anymore. "Sure."

We picked up a moustache and a beard and a pair of glasses with clear glass lenses from a large joke shop, and then she drove me to the *Rue de la Peyronnerie*, a short walk from University Hospital Pitié Salpêtrière. There she parked. Then, with surprising care and concentration, she helped me to put on the beard and the moustache, and even fitted the glasses for me. When she was done, she studied my face a moment.

"You should think about growing a beard, Harry. It suits you."

"Don't get sentimental on me, Colonel. I might get all boyish and clumsy."

She offered me a lopsided smile that was not sarcastic. "That boat sailed a long time ago, for both of us. Go do your job, soldier. Call me when it's over."

I nodded and climbed out of the car. I had the lab coat in a plastic bag. As I walked quickly toward the hospital gardens at the end, I heard the car turn behind me, and the sound of the engine diminish until it was lost in the general noise of the city.

I crossed the gardens and came to the main hospital building. There I walked in like it was something I did every day. The main lobby was crowded with teeming people. I found the johns, pushed my way in, found a cubical and slipped my white coat over my jacket. The stethoscope I put in my pocket and strode back out into the main concourse. I stared hard at the floor as I walked, like I was deep in thought, and walked purposefully to the elevators. The colonel had told me he was on the fourth floor, in the private Fleming ward.

It wasn't hard to find. It was signposted from the elevators. I followed a maze of passages and came abruptly to two swinging doors that bore the legend, *Fleming* above them. I pushed through them and looked left and right.

The private ward was not so different from the rest of the hospital, except that it was a lot more quiet, and there were more nurses. There was a reception desk on my left, a few doors down, and several corridors that ran perpendicular to the one I was on. I looked at the numbers on the doors. I was looking for number twenty-two, but what I was looking at was three, four and five.

I walked quickly, head down, like I had somewhere to be and things to think about, and took the first perpendicular passage on my right. Nobody looked at me, nobody took any notice. Another turn to my right and I was looking at room twenty-four, and just beyond it was number twenty-two. There was a chair outside the door, and in the chair there was a guy who wasn't so much big as hard to believe. He must have been six six, with shoulders you could land B52s on. His neck tapered in to his head, which sat like a bullet on the end. His arms were like legs and his legs were like torsos. Like I said, he was big.

My guess was that he was probably from Ashkenazi's private security. I approached him and he laid down his *Amazing Spiderman* comic to frown at me. On his face it looked like he was trying hard to have a thought. Clipped to his pocket he had a tag that said, "Luomo." I jerked my chin at him and said, "You Luomo?"

"Uh-huh."

"I'm Doctor Brown. I have just arrived from the Mayo. Give me a hand for a moment, will you?"

He looked troubled. "A hand with what?"

"I may need to move the patient to inspect him. Are you alone or do you have a colleague here?"

"Sandy just went to the can."

"OK, we'll get him to help when he gets back. Come on…"

"Wait, you said you're doctor who?"

As he said it I was pushing into the room. There was an armchair on my right, a window opposite and a bed in the middle of the floor. I recognized Ashkenazi in the bed. He was asleep and had a drip in his arm.

Luomo got to his feet and came after me into the room. I laughed, "No, not Doctor Who. That's a TV show."

I turned as he was saying, "I'm gonna have to see some…"

I grabbed him gently by the shoulders, smiling, and positioned him, saying, "Just stand here for a moment, will ya?"

He looked confused, but obliged. There is a simple fact about fighting. However big or strong you are, five to ten pounds per square inch on the tip of your jaw will make you lose consciousness. I delivered a hell of a lot more than that to Luomo's jaw. Then I hugged him and guided him into the armchair that was behind him. When he was sitting comfortably, I took the Fairbairn & Sykes and slipped the blade down behind his left collarbone. He stopped breathing in about fifteen seconds and I removed the blade.

Then I moved over beside Ashkenazi. He must have sensed me there because he opened his eyes. He looked real weak and his pupils were dilated. I smiled at him.

"I'm your doctor," I said. "And there is something we urgently need to know so that we can treat you. Do you understand me, Andy?"

He swallowed and licked his lips, then nodded.

I leaned real close and whispered in his ear, *"The girl gave everything to the killer. So, how do we launch Odin?"*

He smiled and shook his head. "It's too late. Anja knows what to do. Tell Hughes to talk to Anja. And I've been thinking," he added, "in my dreams, the guy in New York, Bauer. It was Bauer. We need to kill him. We need to get that done."

He was delirious. There might be something in what he was saying, or it might be his delirium.

I killed him the same way I had killed Luomo, slipping the razor-sharp blade behind his left collarbone. He had some tissues on the bedside table. I used them to clean the blade and moved toward the door.

When I opened it I found a large, blond man with a handlebar moustache looking down at me. He had freckles and blue eyes, and an expression that said he wasn't as stupid as he looked. I said, "Sandy?"

"Yeah. Where's Luomo?"

"Right here. I'm Doctor Brown, from the Mayo, and I need your help."

He looked at Luomo sitting in the armchair, scowled at me and stepped inside. He stood over his pal and snarled, "What the hell are you doing in here? You're not supposed to..."

He was a good inch taller than me and I had to jump to smash my right elbow into the base of his skull. I felt the vertebrae snap and he fell with a heavy thud on the floor. I thought it was sad that his last thought in this world was about enforcing mindless rules that clearly hadn't helped anybody. It was kind of ironic.

I left the room and closed the door carefully behind me. I made my way to the bathrooms on that floor and, in a cubicle, I removed the glasses, the beard and the moustache, as well as the lab coat and put them all back in the plastic bag, which I had kept in the lab coat pocket. I added the Fairbairn & Sykes and the Sig, and carried them back along the maze of passages, down in the elevator and out onto the street.

There I walked to the *Boulevard Vincent Auriol*, with its nineteenth-century, overhead metro running down the middle of the road. There I turned left and kept going for seven hundred yards, until I came to the Bercy bridge over the Seine. I followed the sidewalk for a couple of minutes, till I was over the deep water at the center of the river, and then scanned the bridge right and left. There were not many people, and none of them seemed very interested in me or what I was doing. I scanned the arches that supported the metro railway that ran over the top of the bridge. There was nobody there either.

So I leaned on the parapet and allowed the bag with the disguise and the weapons to slip from my fingers. It seemed to hang suspended in the air for a moment, and then splashed silently into the muddy waters. There they would soon be covered in silt and lost forever. I looked around. Nobody had noticed, and if they had, they didn't care.

I pulled the burner from my pocket and called the colonel.

"We need to talk. And you need to find Anja Fenninger, fast."

SEVENTEEN

K ate met me at the airport. As I emerged from the arrivals gate she threw herself at me, flung her arms around my chest and squeezed the air out of me. We got in the way of other passengers who streamed past us with quiet huffs and sighs. Finally she looked up, with her deep blue eyes and her wild cascade of red hair, and I kissed her. It was long and heartfelt, and caused more sighs and huffs, and even an occasional tsk!

As I pushed the trolley toward the parking lot, she clung to my arm with both of hers.

"I know I can't ask, and I am not going to, but are you OK? Is everything OK?"

"I'm fine, just tired and in need of a good rest. How about you, Kate?"

She eyed me sidelong. "Have you quit? Really quit?"

"Yes, you know I have."

"Well, I'm glad, because you have some very strange friends."

"What happened?"

"Well, you know I was very groggy from the medication…" She glanced at me like it was something I needed to confirm. I smiled and said, "Sure."

"Well, I woke up in a car. I don't remember much before that. I was in a car and we drove all the way practically to the border with Canada! To a *tiny* village called Machiasport, all one word. I kept asking the driver where he was taking me and who he was, and why they were doing this, but all he would do was smile at me and tell me everything was going to be fine. And not to worry."

"And was everything fine?"

"Well..." She looked at me uncertainly. "I guess. They had a very cute house for me. He gave me the keys when we arrived, and there were written instructions on how everything worked, and who to call if anything happened." She shrugged. "Nothing did happen and pretty soon another man showed up in a car and said he was taking me back to New York and you were arriving at JFK. I was to go and meet you. And that was it."

"Well." I kissed the top of her head. "We can relax now. It's all over and now I am just Mr. Joe Average."

She gave my arm a squeeze and emitted a low laugh. "You might be a lot of things, but never that."

She had brought her car. She made it bleep and I slung my luggage in the trunk. Then I climbed in next to her and we set off across Queens toward the Bronx-Whitestone Bridge. We drove in an uneasy silence for a while. Then she glanced at me and said, "Have you been watching the news?"

"Not much. I've been pretty busy. What happened?"

"You didn't hear? Some kind of international conference in France, and there was a terrorist attack and Steve Plant, you know the guy who created the SearchEngine? Well, he was there, and he was murdered! And that other guy who is really famous, created MyPal, Andy Ashkenazi! He was there too and they had to amputate both his legs, but he ended up dying anyway. And you know William Hughes?"

"Of course."

"Well, it sounds as though he was abducted. He has just vanished from sight and nobody knows where he is. You didn't hear about *any* of this?"

"Some. Snatches."

We went on in silence for a while, and as we approached the water she said, suddenly, "You didn't have anything to do with that, did you, Harry?"

I laughed out loud, though I didn't feel much like laughing. I shook my head.

"No, babe, I didn't have anything to do with that. Of course not. What gave you that crazy idea?"

"Well..." She frowned at the road ahead, like I'd just told her two and two didn't make four. "We were attacked two nights running by men who wanted to kill you. You killed them, and there was barely a scratch on you. You told me this story about your mysterious job, which was very dangerous, we get arrested, I get shouted at by that disgusting Detective Mo Kowalski, and then suddenly we are released, without any explanation, I am driven off to the remotest part of the United States and you vanish for three days to do your last and final job! And what else? Oh, yes, during those three days that international meeting is bombed and those two men are assassinated. While you're away."

I made a face of extreme weariness and said, "Come on, Kate! You can't seriously think I am a terrorist! You're putting two and two together and making five. And besides, if you think about it, it doesn't wash."

"It doesn't?" She sounded almost hopeful. "Why

not?"

"If I was a terrorist, why would the government help me and my girlfriend get off a murder rap? Detective Kowalski was all geared up to invoke the Patriot Act. Why would the Federal Government step in to foil that if I was a terrorist?"

"I don't know." She looked at me sidelong. "Why did they?"

I scratched my head. "I've been around the block a few times, Kate, and I've picked up a few useful friends. Now, I promised you this would be my last job, and you promised me you weren't going to ask about it, remember?"

She grunted as we sped high above the black water of the East River. "I didn't know, when I made that promise, that I was going to be arrested and banished to darkest Maine."

I squeezed her hand. "Well, we are both back safe and sound. That's the important thing."

She gave me a reluctant smile. "OK, Mr. Mysterious. You win. Have it your way."

I waited a moment, then told her, "It's not my way, babe. It's the only way that works."

She nodded. "Now, it's almost noon. We can go out for lunch if you want..." She laughed because I was already shaking my head. "*Or*," she stressed, "I have been shopping and I can make a *huge* avocado salad with couscous, fresh tomatoes, cucumber and fresh parsley and barbecued lamb cutlets. We can eat out in the backyard and I have an ice-cold bottle of white Mendoza and a red Malbec. How does that sound?"

"It sounds good. It sounds like heaven."

Shortly after that we pulled up outside the house.

I climbed out before she did and stood scanning the road, right and left. There was nothing amiss. Everything was fine, as it should be. I pulled the keys from my pocket as she locked the car, and I opened the door.

I stood a moment, smelling the house, listening to it. It was subtly different. She came up close beside me and hugged my arm.

"What are you doing?"

"The house," I said, and smiled down at her. "It smells of you."

"I hope that's a good thing!"

"It sure is."

She gently pushed me inside, came in after me and closed the door.

"Now, I suggest, Mr. Bauer, that you go and take a shower, change out of these tired clothes, get yourself dressed in something comfortable and meanwhile I will be preparing the chops and the salad."

I did as she said. I stripped off in the bedroom, checked my bedside table, took some fresh clothes from the wardrobe and went to the shower. I took my time, switching from piping hot to cold, trying to wash the exhaustion and the sleepiness out of my system. Then I toweled myself dry, shaved and dressed and went out onto the landing.

I heard Kate's voice call up to me, "Harry? Honey? There are some visitors to see you."

It wasn't unexpected, but still I felt the hot burn in my gut. I went down the stairs and stood staring. There were only two of them. They were in jeans and sweat-shirts, and leather jackets. One was sitting on the sofa: six one or two, in his thirties, bald, tattooed on his arms, long moustache. He was watching me and almost smiling. The other was younger, late twenties, short dark hair, clean shaven. He wasn't smiling. I knew them both by sight.

Kate was saying, "They said they were friends of yours. I asked if they wanted to stay for lunch, but they said they couldn't."

Her voice trailed away as she took something out to the backyard.

I said, "What is this about?"

The guy with the moustache spoke. I was surprised that he had a Scottish accent.

"You was with the Regiment, aye? I remember you. So was I. Five years." He jerked his head at his pal. "Gary and me, we met there. Became pals."

I nodded. "So who do you work for now?"

He beamed at me and raised his eyebrows. "I don't know! I get paid, I get told what t'do, and I do it. But, the funny thing is, that is exactly what I was going to ask you."

"Yeah? Well I don't work for anybody. Now if you don't mind..."

"Yeah, that's the thing, pal. I do mind. I kind of really do need to know who you work for."

"Go to hell!"

"I'm afraid not. I can't go anywhere until you tell me who you work for."

I knew what was coming next. I knew because I had been putting the pieces together since I had left for Andorra. Kate's voice came from the kitchen behind me.

"You'd better tell them, Harry. They'll never stop if you don't. They'll just keep coming."

I turned to look at her. She had my Sig in her hand. "I'm sorry, Harry. It comes with the territory. You know that. Just tell us who you work for, and we'll go away and you'll never see us again."

I gave a small snort. "You were good in the part, Kate. Is that your name? But you were just a bit too insistent. You were more interested in knowing who I worked for, than in the fact that I was going to resign. And then you really blew it, when you let it slip that you knew there were two men that night. There was only one way you could have known that."

"Yeah, you're real smart, Harry. So smart that now you have three guns trained on you and no options. Tell us who you work for, Harry, and we'll go away and you get to enjoy your retirement. Play tough, and Scotty and Gary here will do things to you that no human being can tolerate." She winced and shook her head. "I won't even be able to watch...or listen." She held my eye for a long moment, then added, "Because, I guarantee you are going to scream, Harry, and whimper, and sob, like a little baby. Thing is, once they start they cannot stop. They enjoy it too much. So the smart choice is to tell us everything now, before it's too late."

I sighed and rubbed my eyes with the heels of my hands. Then I took a deep breath and said, "I would tell you, Kate. Thing is, if I tell you, I'll have to kill you."

Scotty laughed out loud. "Tha's funny!" he said. "The man's a joker. C'mon pal. On your knees. I'm runnin' out of patience and time."

I turned to face him as he pulled a Glock from under his arm. I snorted.

"I don't get on my knees for God. I'm not going to do it for you, *pal!*"

"Well tha's too bad, then." They both stood. "I guess we'll have to do to you, what you did to poor old Andy Ashkenazi, ay?"

"Woah!" I held up both hands. "I didn't say I wasn't going to talk. I didn't get this far without a broken nose by being stupid. I'll talk to you. I'll tell you what you want to know. But I'm holding you to your word. You said if I talk, you leave and I never see you again." I shook my head and laughed. "I get on my knees, pal, and I know I am never getting up again. I'll talk to you, but I talk from where I can break at least one of your necks if you decide to take me down."

They both looked over at Kate. She nodded and said, "OK, all we want is the information." She came out of the kitchen. "Will you at least sit?"

I pointed at the sofa. "You there. You two sit there and there. I sit here."

I lowered myself into an armchair where I had Scotty six feet away slightly on my left, Gary directly opposite me, roughly the same distance, and Kate slightly to my right. Very deliberately, without haste, I pulled a Fairbairn & Sykes from my boot. I saw Kate gape. I showed it to them and let it rest on the arm of my chair.

To Kate I said, "There are weapons concealed all over this house, Kate. You found the Sig and the knife in my bedside drawer. There are a dozen other locations where I keep weapons." I smiled and shared it with all of them. "I am reconciled to the fact that one day I am going to die. I hope it will be fighting. It might be today. But I promise you all that *at least* one of you will die with me. So don't go getting overconfident. Now, what do you want to know?"

Kate said, "Who do you work for?"

I didn't hesitate. I said, "I *worked* for the Firm, the Central Intelligence Agency."

That was the first lie and they were intended to

spot it. They did. A big grin split Kate's face. She arched an eyebrow and her head tilted to one side, heavy with irony. "No," she said, "you don't."

Scotty and Gary looked at her with an absence of expression that told her she just screwed up. I grinned and the smile faded from her face.

"Thanks," I said, "I just wanted to confirm a theory. You're from the Firm." I turned to Scotty and Gary and pointed at them with the hilt of the knife. "But you're not. You're too good. Besides, you knew what I did to Andy Ashkenazi. You're private contractors. You work for..." I hesitated and shrugged. "Odin?"

They both frowned and looked at each other. "Who?" they said at the same time.

"Don't worry about it. I know a lot more about your employer than you do. So, this means the CIA is in bed with the Einstaat Group and, more precisely, Odin."

Kate asked, "Who the hell is Odin?"

I arched a brow at her. "Odin? He's the god of war..."

"Hang on, hang on, hang on!" It was Scotty who was beginning to look mad. "Just forget the Norse mythology for a bit, will ya! Can I remind you, *we* are asking *you* questions, not the other way around! Quit yacking and start talking! Who do you fuckin' work for?"

I took a deep breath and sighed, like it was more difficult for me than I had expected. During the eight years I had been a blade with the Regiment I had learnt to imitate a few of the guy's accents pretty well. Britain has more accents and dialects than you'd think possible in such a small country, but the most useful one was the accent of the officer class. What they call cut-glass English. I now slipped into it like it was my natural way of speaking and said, "I was recruited from the Regiment by MI6."

The silence was so total you could have heard a pin drop on a Wilton carpet. The lie was credible. The accent made it hard to dismiss. Kate screwed up her brow and squinted, like she couldn't really see me.

"*You* are MI6?"

Gary spoke for the first time. "It bloody well makes sense!"

"Of course it makes sense," I said, crossing one leg easily over the other. "Harry Bauer died in Afghanistan two years ago after trying to execute a prisoner. We suspected the CIA were involved and we were also beginning to suspect that there was an unholy alliance between the Firm and what Roosevelt had called the military industrial complex, but today would be the military, industrial, *IT* complex. And it seems we were not wrong. The CIA is clearly in bed with the Einstaat Group, but we needed to prove it. So I posed as Harry Bauer, down and out back in my native New York, and then undertook a few high-profile hits. That got your attention, but what you couldn't work out was who the hell I was working for. However, what really interested us was how you would respond when the Einstaat Conference approached, and you did exactly what we expected you to do. You tried to kidnap me, A, to find out who the hell was controlling me, and B, to stop me from hitting the conference. And that confirmed our suspicion that the Odin group, *within* the Einstaat Group, were running the CIA, had the CIA in their pocket."

Gary said, "What the devil is the Odin group when it's at home?"

"I'll tell you, Gary, but you won't get it and you won't believe it."

"Try me."

I looked sidelong at Kate. "Do you know?"

An almost imperceptible shake of her head. I thought a moment, then shrugged and said it:

"The creators of NanoWare, MyPal and the SearchEngine pooled their resources and created an actual, real piece of hard AI. They created a virtual god, a god of war."

EIGHTEEN

K ate was on the phone.
"We have a problem… Yeah, yeah, he told us who he works for. That's the problem." She paused, listening, staring this way and that. Her cheeks were pink, flushed. "Listen… Listen to me, sir. He works for the goddamn Brits. Yes! MI-fucking-6!"

A longer silence while she closed her eyes and went on tiptoes a few times. Then:

"Yes sir, no sir, he is being cooperative." She rolled her eyes and shook her head. To me she said, "Why are you being cooperative?"

"To save my skin," I said, and sounded like Daniel Craig.

Whoever she was talking to got mad and started to shout. It sounded like she had a hornet trapped in her cell. She tried to speak over the sound.

"He won't come, sir. No, sir, he won't… *He won't come, sir!*"

She hung up and stood staring at the phone for a moment. Then she looked at me.

"They're sending a squad to get you."

"A D Squad?"

"Yes."

"You coming along for the ride, to watch the fun?"

"I have to."

"And these two?" I jerked my head at Scotty and Gary. Scotty looked offended.

"The job was ours. I still expect to get paid."

I laughed. "Really? You were ordered to kill me?"

"Oh, aye!"

"So all that bull about how you'd leave and I'd never see you again..."

"You know how it is, pal."

I turned to Kate. "Where are they going to take me?"

"I don't know." Suddenly she flushed and clenched her fists. "Oh! This is so fucked up!"

I shrugged with my eyebrows. "It's not going to do wonders for the special relationship." I pointed at her. "Heads will roll at the agency. The US needs Britain right now. The rogues will be weeded out. It has happened before. And *you*, young lady, will be on the wrong side when that happens. They will have to make an example of you and your boss. You can't just go around murdering allies, you know."

She turned on me. "You shouldn't even be here! You're a spy in this country!"

I looked mildly surprised. "Oh, but that's where you're wrong, Kate. I am here at the invitation of the Pentagon."

"*What?*"

I laughed loudly in a way I knew was annoying. "Do you really think there aren't agencies within the State, and within the Pentagon, who know what you're doing and what's going on? Do you really think that MI6 hasn't known about Odin since its inception? And do you *really* believe we would not have approached the relevant authorities on this side of the Atlantic? How bloody naïve are you?"

"*God dammit!*"

Scotty spoke up. "They'll take you to the Huntington Woods, I'd say."

Gary nodded. "That's what I'd do."

"It's what we were bloody *goin'* to do!"

They both laughed and nodded. Kate snarled, "Will you two please shut up! We have a big problem here."

Scotty made a "not so sure" face. "You have a problem, lass. I don't really care about Anglo-American relations. I juss wanna do ma job an' get paid."

"It's not on, you know." I said it frowning at Scotty.

"Wha'sat?"

"Murdering a brother from the Regiment. You should be ashamed, both of you."

Gary stared down at his hands and Scotty rolled his eyes up at the ceiling. "Och!" he said, "I know, I know, I know. It's wrong, and don't think I'm happy about it. But a job's a job, right? And you got to do the job. When they told me, 'Oh, aye, it's an old blade from the Regiment,' I says, no way! I'm no' gonna fuckin' kill one of the guys!' Know what I mean? But then they says to me, 'If you don't fuckin' do it, you'll be fuckin' next.' So, hey ho, know what I'm sayin'? Poor show, I know..."

He shrugged. I looked at Gary.

"What's your excuse?"

"Same as his."

"So, basically, what you're saying is that you are going to participate in my murder because your masters at the CIA..."

"Och, no! *Her* masters at the CIA. We were paid

by someone we don't know. Now you said it's this Odin setup, maybe it's them. But we were ordered to kill you by a person or persons unknown, because of all the fuckin' chaos you've been causin'."

They both laughed again. Gary shook his head. "Leave it to a fucking blade, hey!"

Outside a van pulled up. The engine died. Doors slid and slammed. Kate went and opened the front door. Four men came in pulling balaclavas down over their faces. They were all armed with semiautomatics. Kate pointed at me and for a moment I thought they were going to shoot me where I sat. But one of them snarled, "OK, Bauer, on your feet!"

Scotty stood and Gary stood with him. Scotty said: "Eh, pal, just to let you know, right? The contract is mine. You take him where you like, but we come along, and the kill is ours, all right?"

The guy looked at Kate. "Who are these bozos?"

She said quietly, "They're from the partner." But Scotty was talking over her. "Mind yer manners there, Pinky. We did not request your presence here. This is our show. And to be perfectly honest, we don't need you. Yous can fuck off as soon as you like!"

Kate raised a hand. She was looking stressed. She said, "OK, OK, we take him to the Huntington Woods. You guys," she addressed the four newcomers, "form a perimeter to make sure nobody comes close. Scotty and Gary do the job."

Scotty looked at me and gave me the thumbs up. "Least you'll be snuffed by one of yer own, pal, hey?"

"That is a great consolation, Scotty, yes."

The big guy with the snarl said again, "On your feet! Come on!"

As I stood, the guy next to him pulled a set of cuffs from his belt. I shook my head.

"I am not dying in cuffs and I am not dying on my knees. If you want to try, you'll have to kill me right here."

The big guy swore under his breath. "Drop the damned knife!"

I very deliberately slipped it into the sheet inside my boot.

"I'm going to go quietly, Officer, but I'm going to go my way."

"Gimme the knife!"

"Come and get it. Better still, send a couple of your boys. Anyone game?"

Nobody moved so I looked at Kate and said, "Come on, Kate, lead me to my death."

It was a mile's drive, to the end of my road, down Stadium Avenue and finally to Watt Avenue, which skirted the forest. I went in the car with Scott and Gary behind and Kate driving. The four CIA men came behind in the van.

We turned into Watt and parked on the corner of Bay Shore Avenue. There was a blustery wind whipping up sand on the beach. As Kate killed the engine I said, "I am going to kill those four guys in a moment, Kate. You and I had a thing, and I don't like killing women, so I am giving you a chance to leave. Get out of here. And you guys, Scotty and Gary, out of respect for the Regiment, I'm going to give you the chance too. The three of you, do yourselves a favor. Get the hell out of here."

There was a moment's silence. Then Scotty spoke. "Come on, good try, lad, but this is the end of the road for ye. Oot the car!"

He and Gary climbed out as the four bozos swung

down from the van behind us. I climbed out, but Kate stayed behind the wheel. The big bozo with the big mouth leaned in the window. "You coming or what?"

I didn't hear the answer, but I saw her shake her head. Next thing she'd put the car in gear and taken off at speed toward the freeway. I turned to Scotty and Gary. "I'm sorry," I said.

We clambered over the barrier and trudged, like a troop, through the thick undergrowth of bushes and ferns, toward the trees. Scotty was saying to the bozos, "Man wants to die on his feet. He has a right. And I hope we're clear, you keep edgy while we do the job. Do we understand each other?"

The big bozo snarled, "Jesus! Does anybody know what this guy is talking about?"

I said, "Yeah. He says he has the contract. You keep watch while him and his pal kill me. Do you understand?"

"Yeah yeah, whatever. Just get the goddamn job done. This place will do."

We had penetrated into the denser woodland. The ferns, bushes and grass were tall and thick. We were secluded from the outside and visibility was practically nil. The bozos formed a perimeter and kept watch while Scotty and Gary fitted suppressors to their weapons.

I had to smile. I had focused their attention acutely on the fighting knife, and I had shown them that it was in my boot. It never occurred to them that I might have a firearm, even though I had told them there were a dozen weapons concealed around the house. In their minds, Kate had taken my gun, and I had a knife. Now, the four bozos had their backs to me, looking out for anyone strolling in the woods, and Scotty and Gary were busy screwing on their silencers. For a few seconds their weapons were inoperative. I had the luxury of a full five or six seconds. I didn't waste them. I wasted Scotty and Gary instead.

I pulled the Sig, which I kept under the bath, from my waistband behind my back and shot Gary through the top of his head. Scotty's eyes met mine for a microsecond and he died smiling, with a 9mm round between his eyes. I plugged big bozo between the shoulder blades and the bozo next to him in the back of the neck. Then I bellowed, "*Freeze!*" at the remaining two bozos on my right. They did and I shot them too. That's the price you pay for being stupid and obedient. I didn't say I wouldn't shoot them if they froze. I just told them to freeze.

When Detective Mo Kowalski came thundering through the shrubbery with his band of merry men, about thirty seconds later, he found me sitting on a fallen tree trunk, surrounded by six dead men.

"Jesus Christ!" he said. "You was gonna let us arrest them, for crying out loud!"

"What was I supposed to do," I asked him, "ask them politely to hold on while you finished your lunch? You know how long it takes to shoot a man, Detective? Less than point two five of a second. Take a look—those two had about two twists left on the suppressors, and these four were keeping lookout while these two murdered me. If I had waited I'd be dead by now."

He spread his hands in despair. "Everywhere you go, people wind up dead! They even come to your house to die! What is it with you?"

I stood and approached him and slapped my weapon into his chest. "That's the gun that was used to kill them. You recorded the full audio?"

"Yeah. Thanks."

"You picked up the woman?"

"Straight into our arms, but don't get cocky, Bauer. I am still watching you. I do not approve of foreign agents killing each other on my turf! You understand me?"

"I understand, Detective, and I agree. It's what I am all about." I started walking away, speaking over my shoulder. "If you need me, you'll find me at my house, drinking whisky."

"Hey!" he called after me. "How come you lost your accent?"

"Which one?" I called back.

"So, are you British or not? Are you MI6?"

I paused at the edge of the clearing and turned to smile back at him. "That's a secret, Detective."

"What's your name? Your *real* name."

"Bauer," I said, "Harry Bauer."

I turned and walked away from what should have been the scene of my death. As I walked I pulled my cell from my pocket and called the brigadier.

"Harry," he said.

"Did you get Anja Fenninger?"

"No."

"Kate was planted by the CIA. They wanted to know who I was working for."

"I'm sorry."

"I guess I'll have to be more discreet in future." He didn't answer. I said, "You want me to go find Fenninger?"

"No..." He paused and I stopped walking. Then he said, "Take a rest. Take a couple of weeks, or a month." Another pause. "You've earned it. It was a good job, Harry."

I nodded. "Thank you, sir."

I hung up and kept walking.

WHAT'D YOU THINK?

Nothing is more annoying than someone asking for a review, but unfortunately they "matter" or something. I don't know why, but the vast majority of readers won't buy something unless they see that other's already have and had a good experience.

Therefore, if *you* happened to have a good experience at any point during this read, then I would be exceptionally grateful if you would consider taking a moment to leave behind a quick review. Honestly, it can be super short (or super long...if that's your thing), but even a couple words and a good star rating can go *miles* for a self-published author like myself.

Without you all, I wouldn't be able to do this. I'd have to go out and work in the real world...and that's simply not as fun. I much prefer killing people, err—I mean *writing* about killing people...

Anyways, if leaving a review is something you'd be willing to do, that'd be incredible. But even if you don't, I want you to know just how thankful I am that you even gave my work a chance and made it this far. Seriously, you are the bomb!

EXCERPT OF BOOK 4

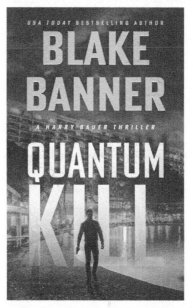

Harry Bauer is a professional assassin. He is employed by Cobra, a shadow agency that provides certain, select Western governments with total deniability, while taking out the trash. Bauer is very good at what he does. In fact, he's the best.

So when the brigadier, his overall boss, tells Bauer to go to Canada, pick up a woman and escort her to DC, he is understandably pissed: He eliminates bad guys, he's not a nursemaid.

But when a few hours into the job the CIA send a highly professional hit squad to take out his charge, Diana, Harry begins to realize there is more to the job than babysitting. And when every attempt to get information about her is stonewalled, both by Diana and Cobra, he knows he has been put in the middle of something big, and dark.

It was supposed to be a simple escort, Calgary to DC, but it ends up taking Bauer and Diana across the Atlantic to the Azores, to Cadiz and beyond, before he discovers the terrifying truth, and does what he has to do, what he does best...

Take out the trash.

ONE

He came at me with a speed that was hard to believe. He didn't kick high to the head. He was too good for that. He stamped with his heel at my knee and as I pulled back he lunged, drove his right fist into my floating ribs, drove a left hook into my kidneys, trapped my right arm with the back of his left fist and smashed his right fist into my jaw. I went down on my back.

He smiled down at me. "You're improving." He said it without irony. "But with you it's either forward or backward. Sometimes you can go to the side, you know? Step left, block my elbow, cross to the ear."

"It might help," I said as I pulled myself off the floor, "if you didn't appear to be in two or three places at the same time."

He wagged a finger at me and grinned. "You know what Bruce used to say, Harry: you have to be like water, fluid, moving, adapting to the shape of your attacker. When he expands, you contract. When he contracts, you expand. Then strike! Pow!"

"Pow?"

He lunged at me again, his fist flashing too fast for the eye to follow. "*Pow!*"

By the time I had reacted he was already doing a little dance, relaxing his arms by his side and laughing. "In Jeet Kune Do, we are intercepting the attack. For that your hands and feet need to be fast, that's true," he tapped his forehead, "but your mind needs to be faster. Your imagination and your fists need to talk to each other, without your intellect joining the conversation."

I gave a small laugh. "How do I do that?"

Again the finger. "*Don't think!* Don't think about my attack, *feel* it." He began to dance around me, ducking, diving, and weaving from side to side. "When I expand..." He threw a right cross and as I leaned out of the way he threw a left, fast. I weaved again. He said, "Good, good. When I expand you contract. Feel the attack. Where is it coming from? Feel it and intercept..."

And there it was. I knew the kick was coming. I didn't think, I knew, and my feet went on their own. They sidestepped and as he drew in after the attack I exploded forward, trapping his right wrist with my left palm and driving a right cross over the top to his jaw.

Unfortunately, by then I had started thinking again and failed to *feel* his left hand grabbing my right wrist, the cutting edge of his right hand to my throat and the sweep that knocked both my feet from under me and landed me on my back again.

"That," he said, pointing down at me, "was *much* better!"

He gave me his hand and pulled me up, talking as he did so. "In war you must think very carefully, but combat is too fast. Your intellect has to shut up and take a back seat. Release the Dark Dragon. You know what that means?"

"No."

"Allow your unconscious, your dark mind, to fight for you. See, hear, above all *feel*, but do not have that internal dialogue going." He put his finger to his lips. "Shh... silence the mind. And when you feel your opponent's attack, explode to intercept it. Allow your unconscious mind to design and lead the attack. That is the Dark Dragon."

"Thank you, Zamudio Shifu, I will try."

He laughed and slapped my shoulder. "You remember Yoda? 'Try not! Do, or do not. There is no try.'"

I smiled. "From Master Yoda himself, huh?"

He pointed across the tatami toward the changing room. "Your telephone is ringing."

I arched an eyebrow at him and crossed the floor at a run. My jacket was hanging on a peg on the wall. I pulled my cell from the pocket and saw it was Colonel Jane Harris, the head of operations.

"Yeah, Bauer."

"Bauer, I have a job for you."

"The brigadier said you were giving me some time off..."

"This takes precedence over everything else."

"Yeah? Why? Says who?"

"You at home?"

"No."

"Then get in that fancy car you bought yourself on the company card and drive to the Minneford Yacht Club, on City Island. There will be somebody waiting for you there. Do it now, Bauer."

I crossed the gym back to where Zamudio was stretching.

"I have to go, Shifu."

"Work?"

I nodded. I had known Zamudio for a long time and he knew what "work" meant. He crossed his legs into a loose half-lotus and wagged a finger at me.

"I do this in the gym, but you do this for real. I know when you are in the field, facing the reality of combat, you do not hesitate or think. You use the Dark Dragon. So why not in training?"

I smiled and shook my head. "I don't know. Maybe I have too much respect for you, Zamudio Shifu."

I dressed, packed my sports bag and stepped out into the New York fall night. Valhalla Drive was dark and quiet. Two streetlamps were visible through the black foliage of trees I could not identify. And out over the water, half of a moon hung low in the sky, tingeing a straggly cloud with silver light. I slung my bag in the trunk of the Cobra and paused a moment to smell the air. It smelt like rain, maybe a storm, but not yet. Out, over the Atlantic. I climbed behind the wheel, fired up the massive 427 Ford big bore engine, heard the seven hundred and fifty horses pawing the blacktop and growled away toward the Bruckner Boulevard. I followed it east across the bay onto Shore Road, and then turned south down City Island Road, all the way to the yacht club.

I found a space to park and pushed through the white picket gate to walk down the path to the clubhouse. The air was rich with those sounds you only hear around boats: the rhythmic slap and clang of shrouds on metal masts, the hum and moan of the breeze through the rigging, and the lapping of small waves against hulls. I believed I could distinguish the sound of wooden hulls from steel and fiberglass, but I also believed I was kidding myself.

As I approached the door a shadow stepped out

in front of me. The guy was big, maybe six-two, with powerful shoulders and a narrow waist. His bearing was military, but right now there was no menace in his movements. As I approached, light from inside picked out the features of his face.

"You Harry Bauer?"

"Who's asking?"

"First Lieutenant Fisher, Marine Corps. Are you Harry Bauer?"

"Are you going to tell me your first name, Lieutenant?"

He frowned, like there was something wrong with me. "No, sir."

"Then quit calling me Harry Bauer. I am Mr. Bauer, you're Lieutenant Fisher. Now, take me to your leader, Lieutenant."

He led me through an empty lobby where a reception desk stood in semi-darkness, up a flight of broad steps and onto a landing where plate-glass doors showed a darkened dining room. They slid open to admit us and I followed him among tables set with white linen to a brick arch that gave onto a comfortable bar illuminated by fat lamps on lamp tables, set beside heavy leather armchairs and sofas. The only occupants of the bar were Brigadier Alexander "Buddy" Byrd, Captain Jane Harris and a guy in a white jacket standing patiently behind the bar. The lieutenant let me in, closed the door and left. The brigadier smiled and stood, with his hand outstretched.

"Harry, very good of you to come. Can't abide all this elbow-bumping nonsense." We shook. The colonel watched impassively and offered me a nod when I greeted her, while the brigadier signaled the waiter.

"Macallan, double, straight up."

She was drinking a gin and tonic. He had a Scotch. I sat.

"I thought you were giving me some time off."

The brigadier sighed softly through his nose and watched the waiter's hands as he delivered my drink.

"Heaven knows you've earned it," he said, once the waiter had gone. "But something has come up which, not to put too fine a point on it, requires rapid and decisive action."

The colonel spoke to the lime in her gin and tonic. "We have other operatives who could handle it, but the brigadier felt you were best suited."

"I'm flattered," I spoke to the colonel, then turned to the brigadier, "I am also very tired."

"I know you are, Harry. I appreciate that. But as I say, this is an exceptional case."

I took a sip of the whisky. "What makes it exceptional?"

He gave his head a single shake. "I can't tell you."

I leaned back in my chair and sucked my teeth for a second. Before I could speak, the colonel said: "This is not a hit, Harry. All we want you to do is go to Canada, collect somebody and deliver them to DC."

I laughed out loud. The brigadier looked embarrassed. The colonel looked pissed. I said, "What, I'm a babysitter now? Haven't you got a couple of tame cops on your payroll you can send?"

The colonel set down her glass on the table.

"If we are asking you to do it, you may assume it requires your particular skills. It is imperative that this person reaches DC safely. We have never undertaken a job of this type before…"

"No," I said, interrupting her, "that's because we

specialize in assassination, not babysitting."

The brigadier looked at me with serious eyes and spoke softly.

"Be quiet, would you, Harry? And listen to what the colonel has to say."

I shut my trap and listened.

"You cannot know anything about this person, either when you go to collect them, or after you have delivered them. That will give you some idea of the importance of this person.

"When you depart for Canada you will be given the basic, minimum information you need to be able to collect the package and bring it with you."

I nodded a few times, glanced at the brigadier, who pretended not to notice me, and turned back to the colonel.

"There is some basic information I am going to need now. If I don't get it I won't do the job. I am not putting my life and the client's on the line in a state of ignorance."

The brigadier said, "What do you absolutely need to know?"

"Is somebody going to try to hit the package?"

He looked at the colonel. She said, "We have removed the package from where they lived and sent them by a very circuitous route to a very remote place where nobody knows them. The move was conducted by professionals who knew what they were doing. The chances that the package is at risk are minimal."

"So this person is being hunted, either to be abducted or killed, which?"

The brigadier said, woodenly, "Probably both."

"Sir!" The colonel was scowling at him with her

lips stretched into a tight line. The brigadier frowned. "He needs to know the score, Jane."

She sighed. "There may be a couple of agencies looking for this person. Some will want them alive, others will want this person terminated."

"The US Marshals, the Feds, they have a lot of experience and expertise doing this kind of thing. This is not my job."

The brigadier grunted a noisy sigh.

"Harry, we are not putting you out to pasture. Personally I think you are at the height of your game. This is not a second-rate job. On the contrary, it could be the most important job we are ever likely to be commissioned. We need you to do it because you are the best. And I can personally guarantee you a handsome bonus at the end."

He wrote a figure on a card and handed it to me. He was right, it was a handsome bonus.

I puffed out my cheeks with un-enthusiasm.

"OK, so tell me why you're hiding the fact that it's a woman."

The brigadier laughed but the colonel looked mad. She snapped: "How did you know that?"

"Because you're trying too damned hard. If it was a guy you'd say 'he' and be done with it. But you can only be trying this hard if it's a woman."

"Absolutely spot on." He smiled. "You see, Jane? He doesn't miss a thing." He turned to me. "It is indeed a woman. We had preferred to give you as little information as possible until you were due to leave, for the safety of the person in question."

"Have I got a choice?"

He spread his hands. "Well, in one sense, of course

you have! But in another, no, not really. We need you to do this, Harry, and we will be very grateful. This woman must arrive in DC safe and sound."

"When?"

"Day after tomorrow you depart her home in Canada. I have given DC approximately a week after that as a delivery date."

"Day after tomorrow? So when were you planning on giving me the sensitive material?"

The colonel answered. "As soon as you quit being an asshole and accept the job."

"Fine, I'll do it. Who is she and where is she?"

"No name. She is a woman. She is staying at an address outside Calgary. You will be given the address when you leave New York. Not before. You will ask her no questions and you will avoid all unnecessary conversation. You will choose the most convenient route, and you will not inform us, but you will get her to DC no later than seven days after departure from her home in Canada. Any questions?"

"Yeah, how do I get into Canada. There are restrictions..."

The brigadier said shortly, "It's been arranged."

"What about coming back?"

"You'll both be provided with American passports and documentation."

"When?"

"It will be delivered to you tomorrow first thing in the morning."

"You say it's up to me what route we take?"

"That's correct."

"What if I want to come in from outside?"

The colonel snapped. "What do you mean? This is

not a game, Bauer!"

"I know it's not a damned game, Colonel! It happens to be my damned life on the line. What if I want to bring her in from Finland or Latvia, one of those low-risk countries."

The brigadier spoke before the colonel could open her mouth. "That's not a problem, Harry. Just make sure you give us time to make the necessary travel arrangements. Some countries can be pretty tricky at the moment. Did you have anywhere in mind?"

"No." I shook my head. "I was just thinking aloud. What about weapons?"

"You can take your Sig and your knife into Canada, but I can't guarantee you'll be able to bring them back. Again, give me as much notice as you can."

TWO

The brigadier needed to pull strings at the border post where I was going to cross, partly so I could get in despite the COVID restrictions, and partly so they wouldn't check me for weapons. But aside from that, he had insisted that I tell nobody, not even him, what route I was going to take into or out of Canada. That suited me fine, though he had also insisted that I keep all communication with him and Cobra down to zero, unless there was a real crisis—like I was dead or dying.

I had been given the package's address at the last minute before I left my house at five AM. I took the Range Rover P525 V8 because I figured it would be less conspicuous than the AC Cobra—or even the VW Golf which I had given a serious makeover. It was going to be roughly two thousand, three hundred miles, almost five thousand round trip, and I thought I'd be glad of the comfort by the time I got there. She was in a small town by the name of Irricana, some twenty-five miles northeast of Calgary, at the foot of the Columbia Mountains.

I crossed the border at Blackpool and took the Autoroute 15 to Montreal. I like Montreal, especially in the fall. It has an old-world elegance you don't find so often anymore in this hive-world of soulless, standard-ized pragmatism, especially in Europe. But on this visit I had no time to do anything but cruise through the broad streets and the mid-morning traffic, headed west.

I followed Autoroute 15 for about thirty miles, through the kind of lush, green landscapes that, if you're on vacation, make you stop your car and get out to look and go "Wow!" And at Sainte-Agathe-des-Monts I merged onto the Trans-Canada Highway, settled back and re-laxed. I still had about two thousand miles to go, two days of solid driving.

Just outside Mont Tremblant I pulled off the road into the parking lot of a Tim Hortons. There was a super-abundance of lawn and trees, and the sky had that rich blue that comes just before the heavy gray of winter. I had lunch, filled a flask with black, sweet coffee and bought a couple of burgers and some chocolate to keep me going for the next eleven hours.

Canadian cops tend to be pretty human, but the speed limits are tight and strict. Sixty-two miles per hour is the maximum speed limit. If you're out on open roads and the conditions are good, they'll turn a blind eye to seventy-five, but if they think you're putting lives at risk they'll stop you and impound your car on the spot. So I was going to have to take it easy and not push my luck, and I did the next stretch of three hundred and forty miles to Kenogami Lake in five hours. By the time I got there and turned north, the sky was turning copper over vast pinewoods, and the road vanished up ahead, swal-lowed by the dense trees.

The next four-hundred-and-fifty-mile stretch would take me deep through dense forest and remote farmland in a large arc, north and then west and south to the tiny village of Nipigon, on the northernmost tip of Lake Superior. By then it would be about midnight and I would need four hours' sleep after a long day.

That would leave me another seventeen or eighteen hours of driving the following day: three six-hour stints broken up by two short rest periods at roughly eleven AM and five PM, arriving at around eleven PM in the evening. I was going to get pretty sick of the Eagles, Credence and Led Zeppelin by the time I got there.

It is hard to follow anybody without being noticed on the Trans-Canada Highway. Aside from the fact that the traffic is too light for anybody to hide behind, the damn thing is fantastically long and straight, so you can't really duck into a side street and come back out a little farther down the road. You're going in a straight line on a practically deserted road, and that's all there is.

I had kept my eyes on the road behind me, and on the sky, and I was pretty sure, as day one came to a close, that I did not have anyone on my tail. That was something, at least. Even so, when I arrived at the motel I paid cash at reception, parked the Range Rover out of sight behind the building and slept with the blind pulled down.

I rose at five, and by five thirty I was on my way again. I drove the first mile with my lights off, scanning the sky for choppers, but didn't find any. At shortly after eleven I stopped at the Hell's Kitchen on 18th Street in Brandon, and drank coffee and ate apple pie among a bunch of Hells Angels who carefully ignored me. Six hours later I stopped again at Piapot and had more coffee and pie at the Guesthouse & Saloon where extremely large men with hands like slabs of granite eyed me sidelong and spoke in quiet voices while they smiled wryly, like life had taught them just about everything worth knowing, and I had been wasting my time in the smoke.

Maybe they were right.

The next stretch of the journey took me into the night, past Medicine Hat and finally to the outskirts of Calgary. There, eleven miles past Strathmore, I took Exit 70 for Drumheller, where the road ran long and straight and dark, through endless fields where lights from distant farms winked, icy in the inky night. Until eventually the few, scattered lights of Irricana rose out of the blackness ahead on my left.

At an intersection with no signposts my GPS told me to turn left off the main road. Another mile through the darkness and I came to another intersection without signposts. This time my GPS told me to turn right. It was like the opposite of peeling off onion skins. I felt I was crawling ever deeper into layers of remote darkness. Another mile and a half, or a little less, and I found myself outside a cute, green and white house with a whiter picket fence and a green lawn in the front yard. Dim light filtered through the closed drapes. It was flanked, right, left and at the rear by tall trees that stood stenciled against a translucent sky with more stars than you'd think possible.

At the front there was a concrete drive and a garage door, but there was no car. So I pulled in and killed the engine and the lights. I sat waiting for a while, looking in my mirrors and from side to side for any movement. Nothing happened till the door opened and a male silhouette stepped out, bringing a momentary glow of yellow with him. He closed the door and shut off the glow, then walked across the lawn toward me.

I slipped the Maxim 9, internally suppressed semi-automatic from the glove compartment and laid it on my lap. I knew who this guy should be, but I didn't know who he was.

As he drew closer I saw he had nothing in his hands. He leaned those hands on the roof over my window and grinned down at me. He was a Swede the brigadier had recruited from Delta.

"Zey giff me a pass wort, but I forgot zee fucking sing. What do you sink about zat?"

"I think you're out of your mind, Jan. You should have let me get out of the car before you came out. I could have been anyone."

"Oh, yah!" He laughed. "Zat is obvious, but I vos votching you all zee vey along zee road wiz zee telescopic night vision on my HK416. I knew it vos you, or you were dead meat ten minutes ago, my friend."

I smiled. "OK, I should have known."

"Vot is zee saying, Harry? Don't teach zee old bitch to suck zee testicles?"

"No." I laughed. "Don't teach your grandmother to suck eggs."

"Sank you, same thing." He jerked his head at the house. "Zis one is a crazy bitch. Be careful. I don't know vot Buddy is doing, but he is playing wiz fire. She is crazy as a box of frogs."

He banged the roof of the car and walked away into the dark. A moment later I heard the engine of a car start up, then watched two red taillights fade into the black.

I climbed out, took my bag from the backseat and crossed the lawn to the front door. The porch light was on. I rang the bell.

The woman who opened the door had steady blue eyes. She had an oval face with a cupid's bow mouth and straight red hair. She had all the features she needed to be a knockout, but somehow it didn't work. There was an expression on her face that said she just didn't care. She didn't even care enough to not give a damn what you thought about her.

She said: "Yes?" and sounded considerably less human than Siri. After close to thirty hours driving, it wasn't what I wanted to hear. I searched my memory banks for the password the brigadier had given me. I found it and said, "I wonder if you can help me. My car has broken down and I need to telephone to my son, Graham, who is an aeronautical engineer, to see if he can help me."

It was, he said, a bizarre enough explanation that nobody was ever likely to say it, but normal enough not to raise suspicion if I should say it to the wrong person. That was the brigadier all over. He spent time thinking about that kind of stuff.

The woman's face didn't alter. Her blue eyes flicked over my features for a second or two, and then she stepped back, pulling the door open with her.

"You can call me Diana," she said. "I will call you John. No personal questions and no personal conversation, please." She said it as she closed the door behind me. "You must be tired from your journey."

I nodded as I glanced around, taking her in along with her surroundings. The place had the feel of a comfortable safe house. The hall was about seven foot across, with a mirror and an umbrella stand and a door at either side, white walls and sage green wood. There was a staircase on the right and to the left of the stairs, twenty feet away, was a door I figured led to the kitchen.

There was no change in her, still no expression in her face or her voice. She was about five foot two, in jeans, Converse sneakers, a violet T-shirt and a lime green cardigan. She had her hands clasped in front of her belly.

I said, "Yeah, it's been a tiring drive." I was about to add that I could use a coffee and a sandwich but she cut in with, "So you won't be much use protecting me tonight."

I raised an eyebrow at her and took a step closer, so I was looking right down at her. She raised her head to meet my gaze.

"Diana, I don't usually babysit women. That's not my job. But not so long ago, after thirty-six hours without sleep, I killed eighteen men and then marched thirty miles through the jungle to an extraction point. All I needed then was a strong, black coffee laced with good Scotch whisky. And that's all I need now, plus a couple of cheese and ham sandwiches. You think you can manage that?"

"I can manage that."

"What about my bedroom?"

"Mine is at the back, overlooking the yard. You can..."

"No." She frowned. It was the first expression I had seen on her face. I ignored it. "If anyone breaks in they are more likely to do it from the back of the house where they are less visible to neighbors. If they do try, better they find me than you when they come through the window."

"Oh..."

She turned and made her way toward the kitchen door. I raised my voice slightly and said, "Oh, and, Diana?"

She stopped and turned back toward me. "Yes?"

"As to no personal questions or information, that's a decision for me. If I think I need some information for our security or survival, I'll ask you for it, and I'll expect to get it."

"That is not what I contracted for."

I nodded. "Me neither. But it's what we got stuck with. You want to get to DC alive and in one piece, you follow my rules."

She watched me climb the stairs. Her blue eyes were the only part of her face that said anything. They said she wasn't happy and she wanted to swap me for another model.

I dumped my bag, checked all the windows, washed my face and went back downstairs. The kitchen was dark. I checked the back door and the window. They were both locked. I checked the rest of the house and found her finally in the living room, watching the TV. There was an armchair drawn up with an occasional table beside it holding four cheese and ham sandwiches and a mug of black coffee. There was also a bottle of Johnny Bauer on the table.

I picked up the remote control and switched off the TV. She watched me sit and lace the coffee. I took a bite of the sandwich and said:

"Here's how it works. Until I hand you over in DC, you never open the door and you never look out of the window. Never means never. If I have to go out for anything and I leave you at the house, apartment, hotel, motel, whatever, we will agree on a code. The way you opened the door tonight could have cost us both our lives. Don't do it again."

"The previous John told me it was you."

"Don't explain. If you explain it means you'll do it again. Don't do it. Ever."

"Fine."

"When we are outside you ride in back. If we are walking you stay close, never more than six feet away."

"So much for social distancing."

I looked for a smile; there wasn't one. "Ideally beside me. In the house you will stay in the same room with me, never more than fifteen to twenty feet away, except when you go to the can."

Her eyebrows rose. It was what she had instead of an expression. "What about sleeping?"

"It takes less than a second to kill somebody, Diana. The time I waste getting from one room to another is the time it takes a pro to slip in, kill you and get out. I am a barrier between you and your killer. You are in the bed. I am on the floor, under the window." I studied her face a moment. I'd have got more information from studying the wall. "These are going to be a couple of very stressful days." I pointed my finger at her heart. "Your safety is my jurisdiction. And if there are people whose purpose it is to kill you, then we cannot screw around with social niceties and sensibilities. We do it my way without quibbling. You don't like that, that's fine. I get back in my car and return where I came from, and you can call the Mannerly Security Agency in Mayfair."

"There is no need for drama, John, and certainly no need for sarcasm. We'll do it as you say."

I sat back in my chair and took a sip of coffee. It felt good. We watched each other for a moment. I was aware that her attention never seemed to waver.

I took a sandwich, bit into it and asked her: "Who is trying to kill you?"

She shook her head. "No. And besides, all you need to do is protect me. You do not need to know anything about them."

"That's bullshit and you know it. For a start if I know who they are I might have some idea of how they are likely to strike. I can get some idea of what resources they have. And, more to the point, I need to know if I can kill them. If they are Russian mafia, Chinese secret service or Sinaloa, then the gloves are off. But if they are CIA or the Canadian Security Intelligence Service, then I have a bigger problem."

She lowered her eyes and pursed her lips and sat like that for a while, looking at her two thumbs side by side. Finally she said, "They are not any official agency. The fact that you are taking me to DC to hand me over should tell you that. The people who are trying to find me and kill me are independent operators and have no legal or official standing."

She was real hard to read. "You don't sound so sure."

"I am absolutely certain."

"So why can't you tell me who they are?"

"Because I don't know. So there is no point in your insisting."

I barked a single laugh. "That has to be a first. Somebody has a whole organization out to kill them and they don't know who they are!"

"Nevertheless."

"OK, so tell me what their beef is and I can work out who they are."

"No."

"I thought we had an understanding."

"And so we have, but that is off the table. I made that clear to your company's representative when we signed our agreement. The reason they are after me is out of bounds. It is enough for you to know that they want to kill me. Why they want to do that is of no concern to anyone except them and me."

I sighed heavily. "So you say…"

Something approaching an expression made her eyes sparkle with anger.

"To paraphrase your own words from a while back, if that is not acceptable to you, you are welcome to get in your car and go back the way you came. It's a red line and we do not cross it."

I nodded once. "If I did that, how would you survive?"

"I probably wouldn't, but the red line stays."

"So you would sooner die than reveal why they are after you."

I asked it flat, with no intonation. It wasn't really a question. She gave a small shrug with her eyebrows. "Draw your own conclusions."

I already had.

THREE

We ate breakfast at six AM, standing in the kitchen, while I made a flask of coffee and she made sandwiches. I was thinking ahead, trying to cover all the angles, without enough information to do it.

"Who set you up in this house?"

"You did." She saw my frown and added, "Your boss, your company."

I gave a single nod and started pouring the hot, black brew into the flask.

"How long ago?"

"The early hours of yesterday. About four in the morning. You people don't sleep much. How come they didn't tell you this?" She asked it looking at the butter she was spreading on her toast. I ignored the question and asked, "What about your phone?"

"What about it?"

"Did they check it? The GPS can be tracked."

She still didn't look at me, laying cheese, ham and cucumber on the bread. "The GPS is switched off. I did that myself when I... When all this started."

I thought about it. She had been here twenty-four hours. Glass half full was they hadn't found her yet. Glass half empty was, maybe they had and they were on their way.

"Where did you start out from?"

"No."

"Give me a break. They may have tracked you electronically. I don't know if they have access to helicopters, planes or bicycles! I at least need to know how much ground they have to cover to get here! They have had twenty-four hours to catch up to you."

She put the sandwiches in a Tupperware box and closed it, glanced at me and put it in a bag. I could feel myself getting mad and tried to suppress it. Finally she said, "Forget it. I am not going to tell you where I came from or where this went down. I didn't tell your boss and I am sure as hell not going to tell you. But I'll tell you this. They'd have to cover a long distance to get here. It is not in this country. That's all I am prepared to tell you."

"The States?"

She shook her head. "Not this continent. If you keep asking I'll stop talking."

I stepped outside. It was just after seven. The dawn chorus had started: a wild cacophony of chatter in the trees. It was still dark, but the horizon had just begun to turn pale. I scanned the street, saw nothing and climbed into the Range Rover, then backed it up across the lawn, as close as I could get it to the front door. Then I went around, opened the back and she came out, hunched, holding her Tupperware boxes. She climbed in the back and lay on the floor, like I had told her. I locked the door of the house. All the lights were off. I put the keys through the letter box and went and got behind the wheel. I locked all the doors and, leaving the lights off, I pulled out of the drive.

I drove at forty miles an hour with the lights off. I kept my eyes on the mirror as much as I did on the road. The lights of the small town of Irricana winked and receded. Nothing blurred them or moved across them. It seemed nothing was following us.

At the first intersection I paused, scanned in every direction and finally turned left. I followed the road for a mile and came to the second intersection. The Trans-Canada Highway was now twelve miles south. I was retracing my steps from the night before, and so far I seemed to be alone. I leaned back.

"We're clear. You can get up on the seat if you want."

She clambered up, gathered her dignity and her Tupperware and sat behind the passenger seat. I said, "Still no lights till we get to the TCH."

"Isn't that the active component in cannabis?"

I sighed because I knew she wasn't being humorous. "No, it's the Trans-Canada Highway."

I made the distance in slightly over twenty minutes, and as I pulled onto the highway, headed east, I switched on the lights, even though the sun was now a deformed, warping glob of molten fire on the eastern horizon. Before pulling out I had checked one last time, and by now I was sure that there was nobody following us, on the ground or in the sky.

After four hours we came to a rough truck stop on the right, and just past it an intersection. Right took me to Piapot, a mile south, where I had stopped a few hours earlier. I checked my watch. It was just after eleven and I figured we could use a rest and a bite to eat.

We moved along a straight road through gently rolling green hills and tall trees. There was something

217

idyllic about the place. Harvest was in the air. Snow was coming in a couple of months. Here, you sensed, the seasons still ruled the year. Cottage roofs and chimneypots peered above hedgerows. There was a sanity to the place that had drained out of the rest of the world.

I heard Diana's voice from the back seat and realized I had been thinking aloud.

"You believe that shit?"

I didn't answer. At the end of the village I turned left onto what some wit in the town hall had called Pacific Avenue, and rolled past a pond and vast meadows dotted with copses. Eventually we came to the Piapot Guesthouse and Saloon and I parked beside a blue Volkswagen Beetle and climbed out.

Inside it was empty and quiet. It was a long room with wooden floors and wooden walls. A wooden bar took up the corner, and pictures and posters hung on the walls advertised musical events at the saloon. There was a guy behind the bar, leaning on it with his elbows. He had a short-cropped beard and dark hair. He was smiling, but there was a touch of insolence to the smile.

"I thought they weren't letting you guys out till the pandemic was over. Seems to me half of the USA's passed through my saloon this morning."

"A hundred and seventy-two million people passed through your saloon this morning?" I climbed on a stool opposite him. "I hope you made a dollar on each one. You got any coffee?"

"I got coffee. I got damn fine coffee. Other dudes said it was the finest coffee they'd drunk this side of the border."

"Well in that case we'll have a cup each, and if you have any pie or something to accompany, we'd be grateful."

"I've got pecan or I got apple. You can take your pick."

Diana said, "We'll have one of each and share, darling." The last word was directed at me with a smile that was astonishing in its sweetness.

The guy with the beard disappeared through a beaded curtain into what I figured was a kitchen. While he was gone Diana squeezed my arm and breathed into my ear, "I'm going to sit at a table. You find out."

I didn't say anything and she went and sat down. The guy with the beard reemerged carrying a tray with pot of coffee, a jug of milk, a bowl of sugar, two small plates each with a piece of pie and two mugs that didn't match. He put it all on the counter and said, "Where you gonna sit?"

I said, "I'll take it from here," and took hold of the tray. "So who were these other Americans? We're here because we live in Montreal, but the border is closed as far as I know."

I spoke as I carried the tray to where Diana was sitting.

"We're all Americans, mister," he said. "You're a citizen of the United States, and I am a subject of the Kingdom of Canada, but we are both Americans, sir." I glanced at him, wondering if he was going to give me trouble, but he was just smiling his insolent smile, and carried on talking. "They said the same thing as you. They lived here and were on a driving holiday. Seemed strange to me."

Diana had poured me coffee and remembered how I had taken it that morning. I picked up the mug and had a sip, then tried the pie.

"That's superb pie," I said with my mouth full.

Then, "Why'd it seem strange? I guess there are a lot of US citizens living in Canada."

"No doubt you're right," he said, "but if you live in Montreal or Quebec, why would you go rent yourself a car in New York? I don't think they'd let you into the USA in the first place, and I know for damn sure they wouldn't let you back into Canada."

I made an "I'll be damned!" face and for good measure added, "Well that is kind of strange." I turned to Diana. "Isn't it, honey?"

"They are obviously on some kind of official business," she said. "What's odd is that they should lie about it."

His insolent grin turned into a chuckle. "Course, I don't know anything 'cause I'm just a country bum, but I think..." He trailed off, gazing at the door. "You know what I think? I think they were cops, hunting for somebody in Canada. And I think the Canadian government turned a blind eye: you scratch my back today, I'll scratch yours tomorrow." He took a deep breath and sighed. "Tell you the truth, I ain't no friend of the cops. Especially cops from the US. No offense. I don't see any reason why they should be hunting people over here where they ain't got no jurisdiction."

I nodded a lot. "None taken," I said. "I agree with you. Were they asking questions?"

"Asked me if we got a lot of strangers passing through. Made me think of you. You passed through just yesterday, didn't you? You were on your own then."

"I did indeed. Did you happen to mention that to these men?"

He shrugged. "You know how it is. You remember something, and then, no sooner did you think of it than you forgot it again. I guess I forgot."

I finished the pie and the coffee. Diana ate and drank in silence. She seemed to be oblivious to me and the guy behind the bar. I took my plate and my cup and put them on the counter.

"How many of these guys were there?"

"Four. They were dressed in leather jackets and jeans. But the way they had their hair cut, and the close shave, you knew they usually wore suits. Know what I mean?"

"I know exactly what you mean. Did they say where they were going?"

"Said they were going west, to Calgary."

"I guess I owe you."

He shook his head. "I'll have a beer and wish you a safe trip."

I paid up and we stepped back out into the mild midday sun. I didn't say anything until we were back in the car, moving north toward the highway.

"New York, huh?"

I flicked my eyes at the mirror and saw her shrug.

"So what?"

"It's not exactly another continent."

"Again, so what?"

"Listen, Diana, you want me to keep you safe? You want me to get you to DC alive? I need to know who—and *what*—we are up against."

"I have already told you as much as I can. Don't insist anymore."

"What do you mean, as much as you can? What's stopping you from telling me everything?"

She didn't answer and I glanced in the mirror again. There I caught her eye. She sighed.

"If I told you that, I'd have to tell you who they are. And I can't do that."

I let it go, but after a minute, when we came to the junction, as I turned on to the highway, I said, "Four guys who usually wear suits, a car rental from New York *and* they got across the border. That sounds like government officials or agents."

"Not necessarily."

"What do you mean, not necessarily?"

"It could be Mafia. It could be private security. Some of those private security companies carry a lot of weight. Some work very closely with the government and are qua-official."

"Qua-official?"

"Yeah, look it up."

I felt hot irritation well up from my belly and had to fight it down. "Is that who's after you? A qua-official security company? I don't believe it. Who's paying their fee? Besides, I know all the goddamn private security companies in New York, and they don't carry out assassinations!"

She was looking out at the passing landscape. She sounded bored. "I didn't say they did, and I didn't say they were after me. You said all that yourself. All I said was, you didn't have to be a government agent or official to get across the border. Or to wear a suit."

I scowled at the mirror. "You are one prime pain in the ass, Diana!"

"Yeah? Tell me something I don't know, John."

"How about you tell me something."

She still wasn't looking at me. She still sounded bored. She said, "Unlikely."

"How the hell did they know you were here?"

"Maybe you have a leak."

I thought about it, thought about the brigadier and dismissed the possibility.

"No. Not possible."

"You're the expert, John. You work it out. I just paid for protection. I didn't pay to be interrogated or put at risk. So why don't you just get me to Washington and quit passing the buck."

We drove on in silence. My mind was racing. Everything was wrong and nothing was right. From the very fact of the brigadier giving me a job of this type— more than that—from the very fact of the brigadier *accepting* a job like this, down to the fact that the client was being taken to DC yet refused to talk about who she was fleeing from and why they were after her; refused even to give information that would save her life. It was all wrong.

People refuse to give information when they are trying to protect somebody. So who was she trying to protect? Was she trying to protect the people who were after her? That made no sense, and yet, what other reason could there be for refusing to name them?

And then there was the whole issue of why we were acting like US Marshals or Feds. We specialized in assassination, in taking out the trash. We did not protect witnesses or escort them into federal custody. The whole point of Cobra, was that we made that entire process unnecessary.

So who the hell was this woman? And who the hell was after her?

At just after two we stopped outside Regina for lunch and then pressed on another five hours through endless rolling green hills and woodlands, until at close to eight o'clock we came to the small town of Virden. There

I came off the highway along Frontage Road and turned in to the Virden Motel. It was dilapidated, run-down and seedy. There was no asphalt parking lot, just an expanse of pockmarked dirt and puddles. I parked round back, where the vehicle was out of sight, and went to the main office to pay and collect the key.

There was nothing remarkable about the office or the bald, portly guy behind the desk. He was friendly and polite and when I told him I was a light sleeper and would appreciate a room that didn't face the highway, he was more than willing to oblige. I collected the key and we made our way to the room. On the way I spoke quietly.

"You don't need to answer me. You just need to think, and I know you can do that. There are just two ways they could have known where we were. One, they received information from somebody. In which case they will have to track us here, and I don't see how they can do that unless they have exceptional resources. Two, they are tracking you electronically, in which case they will come tonight. If they do, then, after I have killed them, you and I are going to have a long, uncomfortable talk during which you are going to do most of the talking. Think about it while we wait."

– END OF EXCERPT –

To see all purchasing options, please visit:
www.blakebanner.com/quantum-kill